MW01717267

Dreams or demons

KEYSTONE ACADEMY
LIBRARY MEDIA CENTER
BELLEVILLE, MI 48111

Eleanor Jones

Dreams or demons

Pony Club

Copyright © 2004 Eleanor Jones
Original title: Dreams or Demons
Cover and inside illustrations: Jennifer Bell
Cover layout: Stabenfeldt AS

Published by PonyClub, Stabenfeldt 2004
Edited by Kathryn Cole
Printing: GGP Media GmbH, Poessneck
ISBN: 82-591-1152-7

Chapter One

Laura Taylor stared straight ahead between Aladdin's sharply pricked ears, her calves firmly clamped around his heaving sides, and her fingers taut on the reins as his iron-shod hooves clattered over the tarmac. When the lane widened she urged him into a canter on the grassy edge. The clatter turned to a squelching thud as his feet sank into soft mud, splattering it up on his belly. But they were too late. As Aladdin sidled past the sign for Hightor and pranced back onto the road again, she could already see the Flynnes' big blue horsebox above the hedge, and it was moving in the opposite direction.

Disappointment flooded over her in a heavy cloud and she closed her hands on the reins.

"No point rushing now, boy," she told the spirited black gelding, but he tossed his head impatiently in reply. His breath rose like clouds of smoke in the crisp morning air.

"Anyone would think you were a dragon," smiled Laura, beginning to feel better already.

By the time they reached the gates of Hightor, Aladdin had settled into a tense walk. Laura reined him in and peered over into the yard, just to convince herself that they really had gone without her. It was her fault, of course; Billy Flynne had told her that if she wanted to go to the sale with him and his dad, Mike, then she must be here by 8 o'clock. Glancing impatiently at her watch, she grimaced; it was almost 8:15.

For just a moment more she allowed the flood of disappointment to linger, then she shrugged her shoulders and reached down to run her hand over Aladdin's sweaty neck.

"Never mind, boy. We'll go for a hack by ourselves."

"I think there's someone else who would like to come," another voice intruded, and she looked up with a start to see the weathered face of old Jim Baines peering at her from over the gates. There was an amused twinkle on his bright blue eyes.

"Missed 'em eh?" he grinned, removing his empty pipe from where it rested comfortably in a gap between two teeth.

Laura shrugged, well used to the old groom's wry humor. "It was my own fault. But *who* else wants to come?"

"The little fella," he replied, opening the gate to let a small black whirlwind escape.

Aladdin snorted, stretching his neck toward the little dog that raced out into the lane, and amazingly, it licked the very end of the horse's nose with obvious affection.

Jim placed the pipe back into his mouth and took two dry sucks before replying.

"In all my years I've never known a horse and dog to be such good friends," he remarked.

Laura laughed.

"It must be because they came to Hightor at exactly the same time. They were both in such a mess when they arrived that I suppose they formed a kind of bond."

The old man nodded, looking critically at the gleaming black gelding.

"Aye, he was a mess all right. You've done a good job with him, lass. Now take the little dog out with you and have a good ride. Go down to Faversham Wood. You'll get a canter there."

Laura had only been to the forest twice before and both times were with Billy, hacking out a couple of his father's horses in the days before Aladdin was fit enough to ride, so she wasn't too sure of the way. But since she had suddenly found herself with the whole day ahead of her and nothing to do but please herself, she decided that it might be a good idea.

"You know, Jim, I think I might just do that," she said with a smile. "Unless there's something else you want me to do, of course. I don't mind staying to help… really."

The old man simply raised his smokeless pipe in a dismissive gesture.

“Get yourself off, lass, you do enough around here. Mind you keep that dog under control, though.”

“It’s Aladdin I need to keep under control,” she groaned. “Come on Toby… heel!”

The little dog scampered toward her to tuck himself obediently in behind her horse, just as Billy had trained him to do. Aladdin tossed his head and snatched at the bit as she urged him forward down the lane.

The chill of early morning had given way to pale autumn sunshine, and Laura lifted her face toward its warming rays as her mount settled into a comfortable trot. For once she had all the time in the world with nothing to rush back to, and she was determined to enjoy the rare occasion.

Funny how things went, she thought, as she turned onto the bridle path beside the river. If they hadn’t moved to Faversham when her father was transferred to England and if they hadn’t bought the old cottage next door to Hightor, she would never have met Billy Flynne that day in the lane; or found Aladdin for that matter. Was that what life was all about, she wondered. Was it a game of chance that led you this way and that, as if someone was playing you like a pawn on a chessboard?

They had only just moved in to Cherry Tree Cottage on that fateful day when she decided to take a walk and explore the lane. She had still felt angry, she remembered; angry for losing all her friends, angry for having to leave her riding lessons back at Burbeck

Stables, and particularly angry with her parents for being the cause of it all. At the time she thought she would never get used to this "quaint" little village her parents seemed to think was so exciting. Boring was more like it. She was an ocean away from everything familiar, even her favorite horse.

She had walked with shoulders hunched, glaring down at the ground as she splashed her boots deliberately into puddles along the lane, then gazing with satisfaction at the muddy mess she had made of her jeans. So, at first, the familiar clip-clopping of hooves on tarmac did not penetrate the invisible barrier she had erected around herself. As far as she was concerned there *were* no horses in the area. There certainly wasn't a riding school to speak of. That was one of the first things she had looked into and, consequently, even one more reason why she felt so unhappy.

It wouldn't have been so bad if her parents had taken the time to understand how important horses were to her, but all they seemed to care about was their "wonderful new adventure" – the lack of it, more like. What would she do with her spare time now? What would she do without Blueberry – the horse she'd ridden at Burbeck? Of course, she hadn't really owned him. But she'd always pretended she did, and now she couldn't even do that. And what about Sal and Moira, her two best friends in the whole world? It was hardly likely they'd cross the Atlantic to drop by for a visit. She could stay in touch by email, but it wasn't the same – never would be.

Laura's smoldering anger had burst into flame and she kicked at a stone, crying out when her toe made contact, just as the clip-clopping sound materialized around the corner in the form of a handsome gray.

"You all right?" called its rider, in a cheerful voice, and her face turned a deep shade of scarlet when she looked up into a pair of warm brown eyes.

She was gazing at a slightly built young man of about sixteen. He had reined in then, and she remembered now how cross she had felt when he just sat staring down at her with an impudent grin on his face. Beneath him the dappled gray gelding had pranced and sidled.

"Had a bit of a disagreement with it, have you?" he had eventually remarked with a twinkle in his eye.

Laura scowled.

"What do you mean?" she retorted.

"The stone," he laughed. "Or didn't I really see you kicking it?"

Then suddenly, unbelievably, Laura was laughing too, and the anger that had been eating at her for days, simply evaporated.

"Can't stand them," she said in a serious voice. "Stones I mean. They're always causing trouble."

So, when had she and Billy Flynne become friends? Right then she supposed. Since that first sentence, delivered in his melodic Irish lilt, conversation had flowed between them and Laura had felt none of her usual awkwardness with strangers. He had jumped down from the lovely dappled gray, on which he sat with an unassuming elegance, and fallen into step beside her as though it was the most natural thing in the world. In no time she found herself telling him about her transatlantic move and her misery at leaving Burbeck Stables, her friends, her school – everything. To her amazement, Billy had understood perfectly. His dad had moved him a long way from his home in Ireland, too. He was only ten at the time, but he still remembered how he had felt.

"But if it's horses you're missing, you can always come to Hightor. It's only five minutes down the lane and there's no shortage of horses *or* work there," he had told her. "For instance, we've had a new batch of ten horses in from Ireland today, and since my dad hurt his back I have to ride them all."

That had been the start of a crazy few months, walking to Hightor at dawn to muck out a dozen boxes before school. On weekends she was flung up onto a succession of half-broken youngsters by Billy's dad, Mike. If her parents had known even half of it they would have been horrified, but as it was they were just glad that she'd stopped complaining and found somewhere to spend her time.

Big, boisterous Mike Flynne just dusted her off when she fell (as she frequently did at first), and legged her straight back on again.

"You have to fall off to learn to stay on," he was constantly telling her, with the same infectious Irish lilt as his son, and she had to admit that before long she did tend to stay aboard when yet another three year old catapulted into the air. And she knew full well that without Mike Flynne's rough education she would never have managed to ride Aladdin. It was all worth it just for that.

Aladdin. She remembered the first time she saw him as though it were yesterday, rather than a whole year ago. She and Billy had gone with Mike to take two horses to Wigton sale – the exact same sale she had just missed today she suddenly realized with a pang of disappointment.

It was the very first horse sale she had ever been to, and it was so much more rough and ready than she had imagined it would be. The noise and bustle had taken her totally by surprise. Above it all, above the sound of frightened horses and humming voices, a terrified, piercing whinny had touched her heartstrings. It drew her toward the corner where a burly dealer was trying to drag a bony youngster into a pen. Billy had forcibly pulled her back.

"Stay out of it," he warned her, but something about the expression in the horse's eyes prevented her from turning away. The "youngster" turned out to be older than it looked. "Rising five and a purebred Arabian," the man insisted as he poked it in the ribs with his stick, but that was hard to believe. Hipbones pressed against the roughness of its matted black coat, it stood with lowered head, its beautiful eyes dull and vacant until anyone approached. Laura couldn't understand why no one else could see that it was fear that drove the poor emaciated creature into a frenzy every time anyone looked at it. Flattened ears and bared teeth were the only protection it knew in a world of misery and violence, and it was that very spirit which made the little black horse so special.

Mike Flynne had told her to leave it alone, Billy had told her to leave it alone, but she knew she couldn't. The hungry, terrified creature needed her and she wasn't going to let it down.

In the end all her efforts had been worthwhile – all the tears and persuasion, tantrums and heartache. Who would have thought that the scrawny, starving animal would turn into her magnificent, loyal, adorable Aladdin? Of course it took months – months of patience and love and care – not to mention the downright hard work she did (and was still doing) to pay Mike Flynne back. And she'd do it all again tomorrow, if necessary, for the beautiful black horse was now the focus of her whole world.

A high-pitched barking burst in on her memories just then, bringing her sharply back to the present. With a start she turned to look for Toby. He was standing in the edge of the lane staring up into a large oak tree that overhung the path. When she called his name again he gave her one quick glance, before turning his attention back to the tree.

"What's up, boy?" she called, reining in. "What have you seen?"

The little black dog's tongue was hanging from the side of his mouth and his button bright eyes shone with excitement.

"It's a squirrel," she laughed. "And you'll never catch it so *come on*... Here, boy."

When Toby whined, following reluctantly as she urged Aladdin into a trot, she remembered old Jim's comments. It *was* unusual, the relationship between the dog and the horse. Funnily enough they had found the poor starving pup on the same day that she had persuaded Mike Flynne to buy Aladdin. She had been in the back of the horsebox, keeping an eye on Aladdin and the other three horses they had bought at the sale. She hadn't really taken much notice when it shuddered to a standstill for a minute. It wasn't until they pulled up again in the yard at Hightor that she realized they had stopped to rescue a puppy that had been dumped on the side of the main road.

"Lucky day for you wasn't it boy?" she told the little dog, and squirrels forgotten, he barked merrily, wagging his stump of a tail.

Faversham Wood was on the opposite side of the village from the stables and Laura took the long route, wanting to keep off the main road, so by the time the trio finally reached the wooden gate that led onto a pathway through the trees, the autumn sun was high in the sky.

She leaned down from the saddle to flick the latch, pushing the gate back with difficulty as Aladdin sidled through to step onto a carpet of leaves. Behind them the gate swung closed with such a clang of finality that he leaped forward. For a fleeting moment Laura felt a cold shiver of apprehension ripple down her spine. The woodland stretched for miles and she had only ever been along the main central pathway with Billy. What if they got lost?

Beneath her, Aladdin shifted his weight from hoof to hoof, tossing his head in eagerness for a canter. When Toby raced off ahead to explore she put her reservations on hold and closed her calves around the horse's black satin sides.

"Come on then," she cried. "We came here for a canter… Let's have one."

The path was broad and straight at first, She allowed Aladdin the have his head, leaning forward over his neck as his hooves pounded effortlessly across the ground, overtaking Toby who raced his heart out in their wake.

When the pathway narrowed, curving sharply to the left, Laura stood up in her stirrups and pulled on the reins, unsure of her surroundings. Aladdin, however, had no intention of slowing down. He fought against the bridle, leaping forward to try and get away again. It took all her skill and strength to bring him back to a controlled canter. By the time she got him into something resembling a walk, they were already deep into the forest.

The first thing she noticed was the silence. Even Aladdin's hooves made no sound on the soft, thick carpet of leaves and she could almost hear the beating of her own heart, echoing inside her head. Way above them the trees stretched skyward, reaching toward the sun. All around autumn leaves fluttered down like golden rain. It was a lonely place she decided, placing her hand on Aladdin's warm neck for reassurance; lonely and somehow mysterious.

A muffled barking deep in the undergrowth suddenly alerted her to the fact that Toby seemed to have disappeared. She yelled his name, turning Aladdin on the spot as she tried to decide where it was coming from. The last thing she wanted to do was lose Billy's dog and she called him again frantically.

"Toby… Toby… Here, boy."

The barking turned into a high pitched whine and then she saw him through the trees, running in the opposite direction, nose down as he followed an enticing scent.

"Toby!" she shrieked and when he ignored her again, reluctantly she turned Aladdin's head off the main pathway and onto a narrow track. As long as she kept her bearings and didn't leave the path, then she couldn't get lost she decided uneasily… Could she?

It was easy at first. The track was wide enough for Aladdin to follow and he jogged along eagerly while Laura's throat became sore from shouting for Toby. Then the undergrowth thickened. Bramble bushes and saplings grew across the path and they had to push their way through, but at least she could see Toby now, just up ahead. He was digging frantically under a bush, whining with excitement.

What startled Aladdin Laura never really knew, but one minute she was peering down at the little dog and the next, the powerful horse beneath her was leaping sideways. She had the vaguest impression of something in the bushes, something large and menacing, but there was no time to think or look. If she had been leaning over the way Aladdin leaped, she may have had a chance to regain her balance. As it was, she was flung sideways, and lost her grip on the reins. That was enough for Aladdin. He raised his head in blind panic, waiting for his rider's support, and when it didn't materialize he bolted, the flight instinct taking over all his senses.

For an endless moment Laura clung to his mane as he plowed through the bushes, deeper and deeper into the forest. At last she managed to grab the flapping reins, every muscle screaming in agony as she clawed herself upright with a surge of relief.

She didn't see the tree branch that hung low in front of them, but she heard the crack when it hit her head, and as the blackness claimed her, somewhere in the distance she heard Aladdin's hooves pounding away. Then she knew no more.

Chapter Two

Rachel Whitmore laid down her clippers, rubbed her palms on her apron, and began to gather up the cuttings that made a vivid splash of color against the gray stone of the patio. Gold, glorious flame, and the vibrant red of berries set against the dark green shiny leaves of holly.

For a moment she paused to gaze at her handiwork with satisfaction. It was hard to believe that this really was her very own garden; in their apartment in the city they had owned only a tiny concrete balcony, with just a couple of flowering tubs to relieve its drab severity. In fact it was still difficult to believe that they lived here at all, how long was it now? Why, she realized, it must be almost two months since they moved into the crumbling splendor of Faversham Hall.

It was a long time since anyone had taken pride in the run-down house, but she and Sam had loved it the moment they saw it, and instantly realized how wonderful it would look once they had restored it to its original condition. It had been harder to convince their fourteen-year-old daughter, Penny, that life in the country had something to offer. At first she had been reluctant to leave all her friends, until she realized that living in the heart of the countryside meant that, at last, it might be possible to have her own horse. That vague promise had made all the difference, and she had moved with almost as much enthusiasm as her parents. Only now, thought Rachel with a sigh, the time had come for her and Sam to honor their promise.

She ran up the semi-circular steps and entered the large, square hall, absorbing the atmosphere, just as she had the very first time she walked through the front door. A kind of sadness hung in the air. Not a scary sadness, just a feeling that something had happened here, some long-ago tragedy perhaps. She was determined to chase away all the old ghosts and turn it once again into a house full of light and happiness, a family house.

Their elderly spaniel, Bounce, lay in his basket near the door, and placing the cuttings carefully down on a small mahogany table against the wall, she called out to him.

"Are you getting too old and fat even to walk out into the garden now? Poor old fellow, I can't see much bounce in you anymore."

The old dog hauled itself to its feet and waddled across to say hello, just as a tall, slim, dark-haired teenager, burst into the room. Penny burst into everywhere she went. It made Rachel feel tired just to watch her daughter sometimes.

"Well, have you dealt with it, Mom?" she cried, crouching down to give Bounce a cuddle.

"Dealt with what?" asked Rachel, hiding her smile.

"The horse, of course! You said you'd ring that Irish man today."

"If you mean Mr. Flynne, well yes, I did ring someone of that name early this morning."

"And… ?"

"And… what?"

She gave her daughter a deliberately vague glance, turning her attention back to the array of autumn foliage on the table and Penny groaned.

"Did he have any?"

Her face was such a picture of excitement that her mother smiled, relenting.

"He said that he had one or two horses that might fit the bill, but he'd keep an eye out at the sale he was going to today… And I've arranged to go and have a look on Sunday afternoon, when your dad is home… *If*, that is."

"If what?" cried Penny eagerly.

"*If* you do your homework and *if* you help me with the supper and *if* you tidy your room…" With a whoop of delight she seized her mother around the waist, danced her in a circle, then grabbed the cuttings from the table.

"I'll do anything you want, starting by arranging these."

"I think that is one job I'd rather do myself," insisted Rachel. "But you can go and get me that nice big vase from the kitchen cupboard... you know, the greenish colored one."

"Coming up," responded Penny.

"And don't forget to put water in it," reminded Rachel, as her daughter raced off down the hallway.

When Penny returned moments later, her mother was in the dining room. She had placed a large sheet of newspaper down on a side table and was busy sorting the vibrant mass of carefully chosen cuttings. Penny watched her for a while, but in her mind she was far away, dreaming of her horse.

"Do you think it will look like Storm?" she sighed, looking up admiringly at the painting that hung above the fireplace. A slight frown clouded her mother's face.

"I don't think you're quite ready for one like him sweetheart," she told her. "I know he is beautiful, but he looks just a bit too spirited to me."

She and Sam had persuaded the elderly woman who sold them the place to include the oil painting that hung above the ornate fireplace. It just seemed right there somehow, and as old Mrs. Haversly was going into a seniors residence, it was of no use to her anymore.

Rachel loved it. From the very first moment she saw it, she had loved it. After she found out a little of its history, she loved it even more, knowing that it belonged here, at Faversham Hall.

The elegant black horse Penny admired so much had attracted her first. It gazed into the distance with shining dark eyes and flowing mane caught forever in a timeless breeze, as it stood motionless in front of the house. Their house.

Its rider sat tall and elegant, her pale face turned toward the painter, and Rachel was taken once again by the sadness she saw reflected there.

"Do you think she really was Lady Faversham?" asked Penny dreamily. Her mother nodded.

"Mrs. Haversly may have been a bit old, but she was very definite that it *was* a painting of the last Lady Faversham, mounted upon her favorite horse, Storm. The story goes that there was a terrible tragedy and eventually they both met a horrible end… not long after this painting was completed seemingly. But of course, these stories do get exaggerated with time.

Penny shuddered.

"I'm not sure if I want to know about that," she said, but her mother reached up and gently touched the painted figure.

"Well, one day I am determined to find out what happened to her. I want to know why she looks so sad."

"Maybe you can get a book from the library on local lore and legends," suggested Penny. "Or you could go on the net. I'll have a look at school if you like… *if* you get my horse, that is."

Rachel laughed. "Well even if we do, I can tell you right now that it won't look anything like Storm. You have to start at the beginning, I'm afraid."

"But you can teach me can't you?" cried Penny, her

brown eyes shining with excitement and a slight frown passed over her mother's face.

"Well I can certainly try," she promised. "It is a long time since I last rode a horse mind you, but to be absolutely honest, I think I'm probably looking forward to it almost as much as you are. Anyway, remember your promise."

Mike Flynne leaned on the brakes outside the gates to Hightor and Billy leaped down from the passenger side to open them, just as Jim Baines appeared from the barn. The old man raised a hand in greeting and ambled across the yard toward them while Mike swung the horsebox around onto the tarmac.

"You're back early," he called as it shuddered to a halt in front of the barn. "Had a good day?"

When Mike jumped down from the driver's seat the smug expression on his broad face told all and the old man laughed.

"Aye, I can see you have."

"You see right," retorted Mike. "Bought three really decent sorts before the sale even started. Then we waited half an hour for a nice bay cob to go through. It was worth waiting for as well, even if I did pay a bit more than I wanted. It'll just do that Whitway woman."

"Whitway woman," repeated the old man vaguely. "What... the same Whitways as have bought the old hall? Are they looking for a horse?"

"Well, more a first pony for their daughter, really.

They're coming to have a look on Sunday so we'll have to give the cob a good try first."

"Sounds like a job for me," groaned Billy as he unfastened the ramp. It creaked its way down to land with a thud on the tarmac and Mike stepped eagerly forward.

"There," he announced with pride, as a bright bay head appeared over the tailgates. "What do you think?"

"Well get him out, then," urged Jim. "Let's have a proper look."

The little horse had all the attributes a cob is supposed to have. Neat bay head with a perfect white star and large kind eyes, deep body, broad chest, and powerful limbs with nice short cannon bones.

"Well?" asked Mike, crossing his arms over his chest and grinning broadly.

"Well… " said the old man. "I think you've found a cracker."

"Perhaps that is what we should call him then," joined in Billy. "Cracker. It's as good a name as any."

Mike shook his head.

"He has a name already. Funny name really, but it does kind of suit him. He's called Cheerful."

"Cheerful!" exclaimed Billy as he led the cob off toward his stable. "What kind of a name is that?"

Jim watched critically as Mike and Billy unloaded the rest of the horses. They were a useful bunch, not world-beaters, just good middle of the road types. The kind of horses a dealer likes to have in his yard.

"So you reckon we've done all right then?" asked

Mike as he heaved up the ramp. The old man removed the pipe from between his teeth and grinned.

"Well at least you haven't brought any scrawny, half starved Arab geldings home this year."

"That's because we didn't take any very persuasive, soft-hearted young girls with us," laughed Mike. "By the way, she was supposed to come with us. Has she been here?"

"Arrived just as you drove off up the lane," the old man told him. "She was so disappointed that I told her to get herself off for a nice long ride. The poor lass does enough around here as it is."

"And has she come back yet?"

At Mike's question the old man's face crumpled into a frown of concern.

"To be honest I was just starting to get a bit worried about her. She went to Faversham Wood with the little dog but that was soon after eight this morning."

"Perhaps she's gone straight home," suggested Mike but Billy, who had overheard the conversation from inside the horsebox, leaped down from the side door shaking his head.

"No, she's stabling Aladdin here from now on because that little paddock beside her house is all churned up. We were just talking about it yesterday."

"Well it's almost half past one now," declared Mike, staring at his watch. "That means she's been gone for over five hours."

Billy chewed on his bottom lip, a worried expression in his dark eyes.

"She isn't used to riding out on her own."

"And that Arab of hers isn't exactly a quiet ride either," added Mike. Then his face brightened.

"I know," he announced. "You can do two jobs in one. "Take the cob out to the woods to look for her. It needs a good road test before the Whitway woman comes to try it and if you go along the main road it won't take you very long to get there."

Billy raised his eyebrows and pulled a face.

"I suppose it *is* good in traffic?"

"Well we'll know that when you come back won't we?" laughed Mike.

While he ran off to tack up the cob the two men fell silent for a moment and then Jim summed up both their thoughts in one sentence.

"I hope the lass is all right."

"She will be," insisted Mike, "She's probably just gone a bit too far." Then his face brightened. "Oh, and I've got something for her as well. You know John Dickon, the dealer we bought the Arab from?"

Jim sucked on his pipe and nodded.

"Well I saw him last month at Penrith sale," went on Mike. "He asked about Aladdin and I was winding him up about it not really being an Arab. Anyway you know what he's like. He got a bit agitated about it, and today at Wigton he came up to me with some papers for him. Billy read them on the way back and they look authentic enough."

"Hmm," remarked Jim. "If they are for Aladdin that is."

"Well I don't suppose he gets too many Arabians in," said Mike. "The lass will be pleased with them anyway. I'll go and get them."

As he walked across toward the horsebox, however, a loud clattering of hooves on tarmac announced the arrival of Cheerful from around the corner. "Here," he called, pulling an object from his pocket, and Billy reined the cob in for a moment. "Take my mobile. I'll ring you if the lass gets back while you're gone… And you ring me if there's a problem."

Billy took the phone and nodded, his mouth set in a firm line as he urged his chunky mount forward and when he trotted past Jim the old man's face cracked into an encouraging smile.

"And watch yourself in that wood," he called. "It is supposed to be haunted, remember."

His advice brought a lighter note to the moment and Billy smiled in response, waving his arm dismissively.

"That's the least of my problems," he laughed "Anyway, I don't believe in ghosts and ghoulies."

The two men watched until horse and rider disappeared from sight. Then Mike turned back toward the horsebox.

"Right then," he said. "I'll go and get those papers to show you."

Chapter Three

Laura squirmed uncomfortably, her head hurt and she felt so cold. Where was she? This wasn't her bed. Something warm was on her face, something warm and wet and… Lucidity dawned.

"Toby," she cried, as the little dog's tongue licked urgently at her cheeks and eyes and nose. His paws were on her chest and her back was pressing against something hard. What was she doing? Where was Aladdin?

Suddenly it all came flooding back. There was something in the bushes, something had scared Aladdin and then she heard a crack. It was her head. The crack was on her head. Gingerly she tried to move and when a pain shot through her temple she sank back into her uncomfortable resting place, trying to hold off Toby's eager ministrations. Was she hurt? Panic rose inside her, fluttering against her rib cage, and she tried to breathe deeply. She was fine. She could breathe and feel… Carefully she opened her eyes… and see, she could even see.

For a moment more she lay in the undergrowth, damp seeping through her jacket chilling her to the bone. Then bit by bit she ran her fingers gently across her head. Her hard hat was still on, securely fastened, and she could feel no trace of blood.

Her confidence rose and she pulled herself to a sitting position, cuddling Toby against her chest while he wriggled to be free.

All she could see were trees and bushes with no sign of the path and, worse, no sign of Aladdin. Where was he? She tried to call his name as she stumbled to her feet but no sound came out and her panic flooded back… but now it was no longer for herself.

The forest seemed so alien, gloomy and dark and unfriendly, a place of guarded secrets and silence.

"You are suffering from shock Laura Taylor," she announced out loud, and her voice seemed to echo inside her head… suffering from shock… suffering from shock. Then Toby barked and normality flooded in. She was lost in the woods, Aladdin was gone, her head hurt like crazy, but she was all right. No doubt she would find her horse grazing happily somewhere close by.

"Come on," she called to Toby, determined not to lose the little dog again. "Let's go and find Aladdin."

She fought her way through the undergrowth, determined not to panic, determined not to admit to herself, even for a moment, that she had any doubts, and determined not to allow herself to think about what had frightened Aladdin in the first place. How long she searched she didn't know. She just kept on walking and calling for Aladdin in the most normal voice she could manage. She had to focus all her attention on finding him for fear of giving in to the nagging ache that threatened to fog her mind.

"Come on Aladdin… here, boy. Hey… hey… hey."

Somehow she seemed to have lost all track of time, or had her watch stopped when she fell? She shook it, was it really only 10:30?

And then she found him, or rather Toby did. He barked excitedly from beyond the trees just ahead of her, and her heart thumped like a drum in her chest when she heard a muffled whinny in response. Eagerly she clawed her way through the bushes, toward the sound.

"Here boy… come on Aladdin."

Her voice rose an octave and she took two deep breaths, trying to keep her tone normal and calm, knowing that any glimmer of panic in her would spook Aladdin. And suddenly there he was, standing motionless in the center of an unexpected open space, head lowered to sniff the nose of his little friend.

"Aladdin," she cried and her eyes brimmed over with the tears she had been holding back. They ran down her face and into her mouth, but she just brushed them away impatiently as she moved cautiously across the clearing, inwardly pleading with him not to panic.

His reins were broken, dangling by his knees, his

neck was damp with sweat and his eyes were wild as he turned toward her, but he was fine. Aladdin was okay.

The relief left her shaking.

"Here boy," she called gently, holding out her hand and he lowered his beautiful head, snorting softly.

"It's all right, you're safe now."

A single shaft of sunlight filtered through into the clearing as her hand closed around the broken rein and she pressed her face against Aladdin's neck, breathing in the scent of him, casting away the shadows that lingered in her mind.

She wasn't hurt, Aladdin was fine, and now they could all go home.

Yet when she tried to mount, her legs suddenly turned to jelly. They buckled beneath her, refusing to obey her commands, and dizziness spread in waves through her head. Fear choked her. What if she passed out, what about Aladdin then?

For a moment she stood quite still, supporting herself against his bulk and when he tossed his head, sidling nervously as if sensing her fear, she knew she had to make him safe while she pulled herself together. If she could only rest for a while she would be fine, she was sure of it. She just needed to sit down.

Fortunately, because she had been on her way to Hightor and Aladdin was to stay there, he wore a head collar beneath his bridle. The lead rope was knotted securely around his neck and with trembling fingers she clumsily untied it and led him, step by step, to the edge of the clearing. There was a tree that would do, tall and straight with nothing to get caught on. Carefully she wrapped the rope around the lowest branch, fastened it in a slipknot, and loosened Aladdin's girth, crooning soothingly to him all the time as the dizziness fogged her brain. Then her legs collapsed beneath her and she slid down the tree, settling her back firmly against its trunk as her eyelids drooped.

Toby woke her. His excited barking reverberated inside her head as she lingered between sleeping and waking, then reality flooded in and she sat up with a start, remembering. Aladdin, was he all right? Please let him be all right.

She clambered to her feet, clutching the rough bark of the trunk and there he was, standing calmly by the tree. His lovely head drooped as he dozed and one hind leg was resting on its toe. A picture of contentment, she realized, with a sigh of relief. But where was Toby?

The little dog had woken her with a frenzy of barking, but now he was silent. In fact the whole forest was silent. She looked around nervously, at least her headache had faded and she felt almost normal again after her sleep. She glanced at her watch with a puzzled frown, it still said 10:30. What was the time? What if the Flynnes were back from the sale? They'd wonder where she'd gone. It couldn't be all that late though, surely.

"Toby... " she called. "Toby... Come on, boy."

Her voice sounded loud in her ears.

"Toby... " she yelled again and then she heard it. A scrabbling sound from the far corner of the clearing, behind a thick clump of bramble bushes. With a quick glance at Aladdin she hurried toward the sound and as she passed across the open space she suddenly realized that she wasn't just in a clearing, but in some sort of ancient, disused quarry. A looming cliff made up one side of it, and the muffled sound was coming from its base.

"Toby... " she called again, but her voice came out in a cracked whisper.

She couldn't see him for the dense mass of brambles. Their cruel thorns tore at her hands when she tried to pull them back, so she lay down onto her stomach and tried to wriggle underneath. She could just make out his small black shape, growling now and digging frantically beneath a pile of rubble.

"Toby!"

Suddenly she found her voice again and the little dog looked around, recognizing the ring of authority. Then he was coming toward her, carrying something in his mouth. A bone, it was an ancient bone. He leaped at her with excitement, his prize firmly gripped between his jaws, and she scrambled backwards against the rough wall of the quarry face, her fingers clawing at its rocky surface.

"Drop it, Toby... Drop it!" she cried, recoiling from the long-dead remains of some poor creature.

The little dog looked up at her, his teeth bared in a doggy smile as the bone fell to his feet. To her surprise his hackles rose, a low growl rumbled in his throat, and he scampered several yards away before stopping to look back with a worried expression in his bright eyes.

"Toby," she called. "What is it, boy?"

Bit-by-bit he came creeping back, his stomach on the forest floor, emitting low growls as he faced his fears.

"There's nothing there, Toby," laughed Laura, following his worried gaze to the cliff behind her. She stepped back with a start as she saw the rough surface against which she had been leaning. It was a wall, a rough stone wall, built in the entrance to some sort of cave. Who could have walled it up, and why?

Something shivered deep inside her, a deep, instinctive awareness of evil, and she found herself recoiling from the place, just as Toby had. From several yards away she, too, stopped and looked back. All was peaceful and quiet and her fears suddenly seemed silly. After all, if there was anything in the cave then it must be long dead. An idea crept into her mind, like a compulsion, taking over her brain. She would get Billy to help her break down the wall. He loved an adventure, and together they would find out why some long-ago person had wanted to seal up the cave.

As she called to Toby and made her way back toward Aladdin, she found herself wondering where the crazy idea had come from, but the more she thought about it the more determined she became. She had to persuade Billy to help her, she just had to find out what lay behind the wall.

In the excitement of finding the cave both she and Toby forgot all about the bone. Heaven knows how many years it had rested undisturbed beneath its funeral pyre of stones, and now it lay discarded amongst the bushes, prey to any creature that might unwittingly come foraging.

Aladdin still waited patiently beside the tree and Laura patted his neck and untied his lead rope, all she wanted now was to get home as quickly as possible, but which way was home? She sidetracked, looking for a pathway to follow, but everywhere seemed to be overgrown, and she clasped her arms around herself. It seemed almost as if she was the first human being to come here since the stupid cave was walled up in the first place.

As she stared hopelessly at the barrier of trees and bushes she felt the throbbing in her head begin again and a wave of helplessness washed over her. All she wanted to do was just sit down for a moment. She knew deep down that it was the wrong thing to do but the compulsion to rest was so strong that she almost gave in to it, and then she heard a voice.

Could it be real or was it just inside her head? It came again, louder now. Billy … ! Could it really be his voice?

"Laura… Laura!"

Billy was looking for her. The relief left her shaking

so much that at first she couldn't reply. She opened her mouth, but no sound came out and for a moment she panicked. What if he went away and left her here?

"Billy!"

"I'll stay on the pathway," he yelled. "Make your way toward my voice."

Even as she pushed her way though the undergrowth, dragging an unwilling Aladdin behind her, Laura's mind went back to the cave. One part of her wanted to get as far away from this place as possible, but some inner compulsion made her stop and think. She had to be able to find the cave again.

Hurriedly she ripped at her shirt, tearing long strips from the bottom. She fastened one to a tree and stepped forward again, following the sound of Billy's regular cries and marking her route with the remnants of her shirt. And then he was there, sitting motionless on a chunky bay cob, a broad grin spreading across his face at the sight of her. It rapidly faded into an expression of horror when he saw the bruise that marked one side of her cheek and forehead.

"What happened to you?

Laura smiled with tired relief.

"I'll explain on the way home," she told him.

Chapter Four

The thunder of Aladdin's hooves seemed to take over Laura's whole body, beating a terrifying rhythm with the heavy thudding of her heart as horse and rider plowed blindly through the blackness of the night; carried helplessly along on a desperate wave of fear. It coursed through both their veins like liquid fire… liquid fear… Horse and rider molded together by a menacing terror they could sense and hear and feel, but could not see.

She leaned down low against Aladdin's crest, breathing in the scent of him as she clung desperately to his strong neck. Sweat-soaked strands of long black mane lashed against her face but she was beyond feeling anything other than the awesome fear that consumed them both, carrying them through the eerie darkness in a hopeless bid for safety.

It was gaining on them; she could hear it… feel it… sense its power. Beneath her Aladdin's muscles bunched as he surged forward in one final attempt to escape the menacing evil that snarled and howled at their heels. In that moment she suddenly knew, with a horrible certainty of raw terror that they could never escape.

"Laura... Laura!"

She struggled to hear the voice that called her name, clawing her way back from the terror that consumed her.

"Laura..."

Someone was shaking her. And then she was falling... falling.

"It's all right, sweetheart. It's just a dream that's all, just a bad dream."

For a moment Laura lay quite still, allowing her mother's words to sink in as reality flooded back. Could it really have been just a dream? She shuddered and turned her face into the soft, warm sweetness of her pillow. "I knew that bang on your head was worse than you pretended," her mother continued, in a worried voice.

Laura did her best to smile, trying to allay her mother's fears, but her eyes hurt in the glare of electric light and she blinked rapidly.

"I'm fine... really. And it's just the bruising that makes my face look sore. It hardly hurts at all."

"Well I think it looks worse than it did last night. Perhaps you should stay at home today and have a rest."

"No!"

Laura sat up in bed, all her fear temporarily forgotten.

"I promised Billy I'd help out today and anyway

Aladdin's there. I can't just not turn up because I've got a little bump on my head."

Her mother shook her head in despair and ran tentative fingers across her daughter's temple.

"Well it's only a quarter to six, so promise me that you'll at least get another couple of hours sleep. And if you feel at all bad, come home immediately."

Laura nodded eagerly. She would have done anything to go to Hightor today, because today, despite the reservations that flooded her mind, she knew that she had to try and persuade Billy to go back with her to the cave.

When her mother had returned to bed, Laura lay quite still in the warm glow of the night table lamp. She didn't dare allow herself to dwell on the dream. There was just something too real about it and she couldn't seem to prevent her mind going back again and again to the moment before Aladdin bolted in the woods. What was it that had frightened him so badly? She remembered something looming behind the bushes then…

She turned on her side and pulled her duvet closely around her, trying to focus on anything other than dreams or invisible demons.

On the way home yesterday she had told Billy all about her fall and losing Aladdin and finding the cave. At first he had called her crazy when she came up with her plan to break down the wall, but she had gradually managed to capture his interest. His final comment on the matter was, "We'll see" and with that she had had to be content. Today she was determined to bring him around, and she couldn't do that if she was sitting at home could she?

Unable to wait any longer she jumped out of bed, pulled on her jodhpurs, dragged a brush through her hair, and cleaned her teeth. A quick glance in the bathroom mirror made her cringe. Her heart shaped face was comfortingly familiar, with its wide spaced gray eyes and annoyingly upturned nose, but her dark curls appeared darker than usual against her pale cheeks. The deep purple bruise was vivid on one side of her head. She touched her fingers to it, wincing as they made contact, and then gently eased her sweater on and ran down the stairs.

By the time she arrived at Hightor the yard was already bustling and the first person she saw as she slipped though the gates, was old Jim.

"What were you trying to do yesterday?" he called. "Frighten us all to death?"

Laura grinned sheepishly.

"Well I certainly frightened myself."

As he walked toward her he swung the haynets he was carrying off his shoulder, then he stopped, dropping them onto the ground as he stared at the purple mark on her face.

"You've made a right mess of that, lass. Should you be here?"

Her mouth set into a firm line and she nodded, trying to ignore the dull thudding in her head.

"I'm fine… really. It's just superficial."

Jim frowned, shaking his head from side to side.

"Well you be careful. I'm a silly old fool who should never have told you to go to the wood in the first place."

"What? Are you admitting to being a silly old fool, Jim Baines?"

At the sound of Mike Flynne's voice they both looked round with a start to see his broad figure standing behind them. His dark eyes, as always, held a glimmer of amusement, and his face was stretched into a satisfied smile as he rocked back on his heels with fingers tucked into his belt.

"Never thought I'd hear that," he went on.

Jim's initial scowl turned into a chuckle.

"There's no fool like an old fool, Mike, you should know that," he remarked, with a meaningful glance. Mike just laughed and turned his attention to Laura.

"It wouldn't have happened if you'd come to Wigton with us," he told her, then his face cracked into a smile. "But at least I wasn't forced into buying any scrawny Arabians this year. Now you let me know if you don't feel well, lass."

Laura nodded.

"I'm fine, honestly. I'll go and get started."

"Billy's done the six boxes by the tack room," he called after her as she turned to walk away. "Oh, and by the by, I've got something for you."

He withdrew what looked like an envelope from his pocket and held it out toward her.

"I saw John Dickon yesterday. You know, the dealer who had Aladdin in the first place?"

The breath caught in Laura's throat as her fingers closed around the cream envelope.

"Well, I've had him on once or twice about the horse not really being a registered Arab. I mean it's hardly the type of horse he usually deals in, and to be honest, I'd have bet a hundred pounds that it was only a part bred. Not that he doesn't look like an Arab," he added hurriedly, when he saw the expression on Laura's face.

"Anyway, believe it or not, he turned up yesterday with a registration document for the horse. It looks authentic enough to me. See what you think."

"Thanks."

Laura gave Mike a broad smile, hugging the papers against her chest, longing to look at them.

"I'll read them through when I've finished mucking out," she said, and he laughed.

"I'll bet you can't wait that long."

Billy found her in Cheerful's box. The chunky bay cob had his face stuffed into a hay net, snorting happily as he chewed, and Laura was madly forking soiled straw into her barrow. She still hadn't looked at the document that was safely tucked into her inside pocket. "Just one more box to go," she kept telling herself.

"I've been thinking about yesterday."

His voice made her jump. She dropped her fork and turned toward the sound, running her fingers through her short mop of curls as she stared at the figure outlined in the doorway.

"And… What have you thought about?"

"I think it might be a laugh."

Laura felt a kind of glow ripple through her, and inwardly recoiled from it. Why was it so important to her to get into the cave, anyway? She dismissed her niggling doubts instantly.

"We might make a great discovery."

"We might put in a lot of hard work for absolutely nothing, more like." He laughed. "Anyway, no one calls me a spoil sport. We'll go tomorrow lunchtime, since there's no school, or as soon as we've finished off, and to stop my dad moaning, we'll take out the two geldings from Wigton. Two jobs in one, so to speak. They get a good hack and a try on the roads, and we tie them up and spend half an hour trying to knock down your ridiculous wall. I still think you're mad, though."

His broad grin, however, belied the comment and Laura smiled back.

"I think that you are just as excited me," she retorted.

Billy shrugged.

"We have to be back before 3:00, though, because someone is coming to try the cob and I'll have to ride it for them."

"Oh, not poor Cheerful."

Laura patted the bay's broad rump with a rush of pity, but Billy shook his head.

"I wouldn't feel sorry for him. It sounds like a really good home, you know, first horse and all that. He'll be doted on."

He was already walking away by the time Laura remembered that she hadn't mentioned Aladdin's registration documents and she almost called him back. Then, changing her mind, she picked up her fork again. She would read them through herself when she went to muck him out. That seemed appropriate, and Billy could look at them later.

She left Aladdin's box until the end, and as she slid the bolt on his door he tossed his lovely head impatiently.

"Last, but definitely not least," she told him, tying his lead rope to the ring beside the manger. "How was your first night here, boy? Was it nice to have company?" She quickly mucked him out, straightened his rug, and picked out his feet before finally pulling the papers from her pocket. He snorted over her shoulder and she laughed, holding them up to his nose.

"Do you want to see? Well listen, and I'll read them out to you."

The document was much as she expected, a kind of family tree culminating with Aladdin.

"And not *just* Aladdin, but *Hallbank* Aladdin," she read. "I wonder where Hallbank is… Well, he was honest about your age anyway; this makes you five years old… and listen to your parents' names. Now they really are fancy. Your dam is Hallbank Indian Magic, your sire is Free Spirit and your grandsire... your grandsire is Spirit of Fire."

Aladdin nudged her in the back then, more concerned with getting his breakfast than listening to his owner's ramblings and she gave him a pat on the neck before folding the document up to slide it carefully back into her pocket.

"All right," she said, smiling. "I'll read the rest later, but it is nice to know where you came from, don't you think?

Aladdin's response was to blow through his nostrils, snuffling softly against her and she pressed her cheek against the smooth black velvet of his nose.

"I really don't care who you are, you know, she told him. "Now let's get your feed."

Over a breakfast of bacon and eggs, Mike and Billy read through Aladdin's papers.

"There's some good breeding in here," remarked Mike as he buttered yet another slice of toast.

"This sire line, you know, all the Spirits, I've seen them in the Horse and Hound loads of times. Thing is, however did John Dickon get hold of him?"

"I suppose that's something we'll never know," remarked Billy.

"The main thing," added Laura. "Is that he did get hold of him."

"And that you happened to come to Wigton with us last year," joined in Mike. "Because one thing is for sure, I'd never have bought him if you hadn't begged me."

Billy's mother, Jenny, looked up from the stove just then, her round face pink with the heat.

"It's fate," she said determinedly. "It was meant to be."

"Rubbish," snorted Mike. "You make your own fate."

Jenny simply smiled and shook her head.

"Please yourself," she said with a shrug. "But I still believe it was fate."

A funny tingle rippled down Laura's spine.

"So do you suppose it was fate that made me miss going to Wigton yesterday?" she asked. Jenny merely laughed and began clearing the breakfast dishes.

"Perhaps."

"And went all alone into a haunted wood," cried Billy in a spooky voice.

"Now that's enough," announced Mike. "You'll be frightening the lass half to death with your daft ideas. Come on, there's work to be done."

The afternoon flew by and it wasn't until she was walking home along the lane that Laura remembered Jenny's comments at breakfast about fate and such. It made her feel uneasy to think that perhaps there was a purpose to her missing the sale, and she didn't dare allow herself to dwell on Billy's joking comments about the forest being haunted. Faversham Wood held too many scary memories for her already; in fact she couldn't understand why she had persuaded Billy to go with her to the cave tomorrow at all. She really must be crazy.

Dusk was falling and she hurried her steps, suddenly eager to leave the lengthening shadows behind her. The warm beams of light, shining out from the windows of Cherry Tree Cottage, had never seemed more welcome. The back door latch made a familiar click beneath her fingers and when she stepped into the kitchen she was met by a warm blast of air, heavy with the succulent aroma of a roast cooking. It felt good to be home.

"About time, too," scolded her mother. "I was just getting worried about you. Come on, get cleaned up, your father will be home any minute, and I'm sure he doesn't want to smell horses all over the place."

Laura stayed awake that night for as long as she could, fending off sleep, afraid that the nightmare would return again. She kept her bedside lamp switched on, taking confidence from its warm light and when she awoke, just as dawn was breaking, it's yellow glow still lit up her small, comfortable room. For a while she lay quite still, staring at the cracked shapes on the ceiling. The night was over. All she had to do now was go to the cave with Billy, and that would be fun… wouldn't it? Who knows what they might find.

On the short walk to Hightor she tried to raise some enthusiasm for the plan ahead, and by the time she reached the yard she was almost looking forward to it. The gates swung shut behind her with a click as the catch made contact, and she saw Billy over by the stable block. He was just about to mount the brown and white jumping stallion, Paint, and she paused to watch as he carefully slid into the saddle and found his stirrups. Then he gathered up the reins and walked the big horse toward her.

"Ready for our adventure?" he called.

Laura answered with a broad grin.

"Well, I'm as ready as I'll ever be, but I still think it's going to be a waste of time. If there was ever anything in that cave, then someone would have broken in and found it years ago."

"To be honest I hope you're right," admitted Laura and he laughed at the sudden apprehension on her face.

"Laura Taylor I do believe you're scared," he cried. "Do you want to change your mind? We don't have to go, you know."

Laura's response was instant.

"Don't be silly. I'm looking forward to it."

Billy clicked under his tongue and Paint darted forward.

"Better get a move on, then," he told her in a serious tone but she didn't miss the amused twinkle in his eyes.

Laura worked as quickly as she could, eager to get to Aladdin's box and, as before, leaving him until last. That way she could get to spend longer on him than the others. This morning, however, time was short and Billy was already calling her to breakfast as she slipped on his head collar.

“You go ahead,” she called back. “Start without me.”

As soon as she approached his stable door she had known that something was wrong. He was staring out toward the hills beyond the stable yard, red lined nostrils flaring and huge, dark eyes wide with tension. She held out her hand with a piece of carrot, speaking to him in a low, gentle tone, but for once he totally ignored her.

“What is it, boy?” she crooned as he tossed his beautiful head, then he raced round his box and came back to the half door, stretching his neck to stare once again into the distance.

By the time she had managed to slip on his head collar and tie his lead rope to the ring at the back of the box, he seemed to settle down a little, and she spent a few minutes rubbing his ears and talking to him, until he was relaxed enough to take some pieces of carrot from her hand. Then she quickly mucked him out, fetched his feed and finally left him to eat it, still wary, but at least a bit more settled now.

She mentioned his behavior to Billy over breakfast, expecting him to laugh at her fears, but a frown of concern flitted across his forehead.

“I hope there hasn’t been anyone sneaking around in the night,” he said. “We always have to keep an eye out, you know. There are plenty of things to steal around here. I’ll mention it to my dad. Why don’t you turn Aladdin out in the far paddock for a couple of hours, while we go to the wood, that will do him as much good as anything."

"Thanks," responded Laura. "Good idea." But the niggle of worry remained. She hadn't seen her precious horse so upset since those early days when he trusted no one.

They left for Faversham wood at lunchtime, mounted upon the two chestnuts from Wigton. Laura's was a sturdy, sixteen hand gelding with a big plain head and a lovely honest face. Billy's was a bright piebald, with four white socks and broad white blaze. It pranced out of the yard, sticking its tail in the air and snorting when they passed the meadow where Aladdin was turned out. Laura's mount plodded behind, totally unconcerned when the elegant black gelding took off across the meadow at full gallop, bucking and leaping.

"Well, he seems all right now," remarked Billy with a grin, as his horse cavorted along the lane.

They settled into an easy silence, broken only by the occasional comment.

"I see you've brought a pick," remarked Laura.

"And a torch, or a flashlight as you insist on calling it," laughed Billy. "We are definitely going to get into this cave of yours, even if it is a waste of time." As they rode through the gate into Faversham Wood, into the powerful looming silence of the trees, Laura felt the breath freeze in her throat and she glanced across at Billy. Did he feel it too?

He was staring straight ahead, eager to get on, his face bright with anticipation.

"Billy," she called, but her voice came out in a whisper.

He reined in and looked back, his eyes dark with impatience.

"Yes?"

"Oh, nothing..." she murmured, urging her horse forward to catch up.

Chapter Five

"So what time are we leaving?"

With an exasperated sigh Rachel Whitway put down the pile of ironing she was folding and turned to look at her daughter, who was sitting on the window seat staring out into the murky gray autumn sky.

"Penny!" she exclaimed. "That's the third time you've asked me that question in the last hour, and you know the answer perfectly well. It's only a twenty-minute drive to Hightor so we don't need to leave until almost half past two. Anyway, we can't go until your dad comes home, so you'd better hope he isn't late. And of course," she added with a smile. "I can always find you something to do if you're bored."

Penny untangled her long legs from beneath her and clambered to her feet. "I've just thought of a very useful job," she announced, reaching for the lead that hung on a hook near the door. "I'll take Bounce for a walk."

"Well, Bounce might not agree," remarked her mother, as the elderly dog heaved itself reluctantly into a sitting position. "But it will certainly do him good. Off you go then, and keep an eye out for Dad."

Penny walked along the side of the house into the rambling wilderness of the back garden, clutching her reluctant partner's lead securely in her hand. Excitement bubbled up inside her, pushing her heart-beat into her throat. She found herself wondering how she was going to manage to wait any longer before she got to see her horse. In her mind's eye it always looked like Storm, kind of wild and elegant and totally magnificent, but in truth she knew different.

"I don't care what it looks like anyway," she informed a totally disinterested Bounce. "It will still be my best friend… apart from you, of course. Now come on, where do you want to go? And I don't mean home."

Rachel Whitway had made great progress on the front garden at Faversham Hall, but the massive area at the rear of the house had remained totally untouched for years. It stretched to the river on one side and on the other it was skirted by the dense mass of Faversham Wood, which to Penny seemed like merely an extension of the garden, as there was a small gate that lead directly onto the main pathway through the trees.

She often walked Bounce that way, just as far as the gate that led back onto the lane, but she had never dared to venture any farther into the trees. There was something about the wood. Something melancholy and sad and slightly scary. It had made her wary even before her father laughingly told her that it was supposed to be haunted. After that, nothing would have made her take one step off the short familiar route, even though she was pretty sure that he was only joking.

"Come on Bounce," she urged, leaving the cold gray misty air of the garden for the gloomy silence of the trees and as the gate closed behind her she glanced around uneasily. Silence… that is what it was. That was what made the place feel so lonely and kind of eerie.

Taking a deep breath she stepped determinedly forward with Bounce at her heels. The air smelled of wood and earth and something else, some herby fragrance. She breathed it in as she walked along the pathway, humming to herself to fend off the clinging silence.

When the sound first started she wasn't sure, for it seemed to blend with the feel of the woodland like a distant beating heart. She paused, pulling back to the edge of the trees as the sound grew louder. Suddenly, with a surge of both excitement and relief, she realized what it was. Hooves, it was the sound of horses' hooves. Someone was riding through the forest.

Just as she stepped out onto the pathway again, eager to see who it was, two chestnut horses appeared from around the corner. The first was a rich, bright red, with four white socks that almost sparkled as they danced across the dark leaf-strewn ground. It rolled its eyes and sidled when it saw her and its rider, a boy of about sixteen, gave her a wide, friendly grin.

The second horse was a much chunkier, darker, liver chestnut. It ambled in the wake of its spirited companion, and at first Penny didn't notice the slightly-built girl who rode it, until she spoke.

"Hello… Nice dog."

Did she mean Bounce? Penny looked up, confusion flooding her face and the girl smiled. Her wide spaced gray eyes seemed honest and friendly, and her elfin features made Penny feel suddenly gauche and awkward.

"He's getting a bit old," she mumbled.

"Unlike Toby," warned the girl, as a small black whirlwind leaped from the undergrowth and proceeded to jump all over poor Bounce. When Penny knelt down to pry its playful teeth from the spaniel's temptingly dangly ears, the boy on the bright chestnut called out to him in a firm, authoritative tone.

"Toby… Heel!"

Amazingly the little dog pricked its ears and, with one last sharp bark, dashed off obediently to fall in behind his horse.

"See you," called the girl, as her companion broke into a trot, then she legged her reluctant mount forward and cantered off in his wake.

For a moment Penny stood watching as the horses moved away through the trees. Maybe that would soon be her; maybe she would soon be cantering through the woodland, breaking the silence with the gentle thud of hoof beats, her horse's ears pricked before her as she urged him forward.

When a vague awareness of movement in the undergrowth cut in on her thoughts, her dream evaporated, to be replaced by the slightest prickle of alarm. Something loomed beyond the trees… and then it was gone. Her heart quickened. It must be, had to be, a shadow. Gathering up the lead she urged Bounce onto his feet, glancing reluctantly back. There it was again, just an impression, a vague, formless impression of a large dark shape moving through the undergrowth. And then the horses disappeared from sight, and suddenly it too, was gone. Had she imagined it?

She shuddered, breaking into a jog, eager to be home, and by the time she reached the gates to Faversham Hall she had already discounted the incident. Imagination is all it was, just her active imagination.

She climbed the curved steps to the front door, and to her delight, her father's sleek black car appeared in the drive. She let Bounce into the house, then stopped to wait for him. The car tires crunched to a halt on the gravel and he climbed out of the driver's side, all smiles and good humor.

"Well, are you excited?" he asked, withdrawing his briefcase and a slim brown parcel from the back seat.

"What do you think?" responded Penny.

His green eyes met hers and held for a moment.

"I think you are probably a bit nervous."

"But excited as well," added Penny. "Have you brought me a present?"

Her father glanced down at the parcel.

"Sort of. Well, it's for your mother really, but it kind of affects you too, I suppose."

"Come on," cried Penny, grabbing his arm. "Let's go and give it to her."

"A present!" exclaimed Rachel Whitway, when her husband handed her the brown paper parcel. She hurriedly ripped it open, her round face pink with anticipation.

"It's a book!" exclaimed Penny.

"A very old-looking book," added her mother, turning it over to read the title.

The book had once been bound in dark brown leather, its pages tipped with gold, but now its spine was torn and the leather was scuffed and ripped in places.

"Myths and Legends of Fairburn and Faversham," read Rachel with a broad smile.

"Where on earth did you get it?"

"My fan belt was slipping so I stopped at that little garage in Fairburn to get it fixed. While I was waiting, I found the funniest little shop down a side street near the traffic lights. It sold all sorts of odd things, but I just kind of stumbled on the book. Anyway, I remembered how you are always going on about that painting and the last Lady Faversham and that horse of hers, Storm. I thought maybe her story would be in it. I mean it has to be a local myth or legend, doesn't it?"

"Perhaps it will tell us what haunts Faversham Wood," cried Penny, suddenly remembering the shapeless form in the trees.

"That," remarked her father, "is a little too close to home. Now come on, girls, you can read it later. Off you go and get ready. It's time we went to see about a horse."

Deep in the forest, by unspoken, mutual consent, Billy and Laura reined in. The white-faced chestnut chomped on its bit, prancing impatiently, but Laura's placid mount merely yanked at the bit and dived down for grass.

"Get up, lad," she cried, her heels beating a tattoo on its well-covered rib cage, and the gelding obliged by walking reluctantly forward. Then suddenly she saw it. A tiny white speck attached to a tree.

I told you I could find it again," she cried, her eyes bright with excitement.

"Worst luck," groaned Billy. "I thought your bits of cloth would be blown away by now. Anyway, you still have to try and get through that undergrowth to reach the clearing."

Laura frowned.

"Well I managed to drag Aladdin through, so I suppose it is possible."

"Yes but you were a bit desperate at the time," remarked Billy, vaulting lightly to the ground and removing the long wooden handle of the pick from where it was slotted neatly onto his saddle. He wielded its fearsome point at the nearest bramble bush and when his horse shied away from it he paused for a moment, frowning.

"I tell you what," he suggested. "Why don't we leave the horses tied up here and I'll hack a way through?"

"That," declared Laura, already dismounting. "Is one of your better ideas."

By the time they had fought through the undergrowth, following Laura's trail, they both began to wonder how she had found her way into the clearing in the first place.

"It must have been undisturbed for years," declared Billy.

"Probably since the cave was first walled up," suggested Laura.

The same thought passed through both their minds then, but neither of them dared to put it into words. What if no one had come here for a reason? What if the cave held some long-kept secret? And as the trees thinned out, they moved closer together, needing the comfort of touch but unwilling to admit it.

"Where is it?" murmured Billy, unaware that he was whispering, and Laura pointed toward a thick clump of brambles that grew close against the wall of the cliff.

"There. I only found it because I had to try and drag Toby out."

"Where is Toby?"

And then they saw him, running toward them, his eyes bright with excitement and his jaws firmly clamped around a long pale object.

"Drop it," ordered Billy and the dog duly obliged,

wagging his stump of a tail so hard that his whole backside wriggled.

"It's that disgusting bone again," declared Laura. "He found it the other day. That's what he was digging for in the first place.

Billy poked the object with his toe then leaned down and picked it up between thumb and forefinger.

"It's a horse's bone!" he exclaimed, holding it out to her. "Look, I think it's a cannon bone. You can still see where the splint bones were attached."

Laura shrank away from it.

"Put it down," she insisted, but Billy merely laughed.

"Dead bones can't hurt you," he told her. "And this one must have been dead for… who knows… maybe a couple of hundred years or more. Where did he find it, anyway?"

Laura pointed to the pile of rocks behind the brambles, where Toby had been digging. They were overgrown now with weeds and moss, but must at some time have fallen down the cliff face.

"You see," declared Billy. "If the horse was buried under those rocks then its bones could have easily been preserved."

Laura shuddered.

"Never mind ancient bones," she begged. "Let's just get on with it and go home."

Billy was intrigued when he saw the cave.

"Obviously someone walled it up," he agreed. "But I wouldn't worry. As I told you before, it must have been done over a hundred years ago, maybe more. If there were any secrets here then I'm sure someone would have found them by now. You are not seriously trying to tell me that you are the first person to find it in all this time are you?"

Laura's response was to step back, laughing just a little too loudly as Billy raised his pick.

Once… twice… three times he struck the crudely-built wall before the stones began to move, and when the first tiny gap appeared Laura felt a draught of air so icy cold against her cheek that she gasped with shock.

She wanted to yell at him to stop, wanted to tell him to forget that she'd ever seen the cave in the first place, but instead she just stood in frozen silence as the stones came clattering down. And as the gap widened something seeped into her bones, an intangible, clinging fear of an evil she could only sense.

"There," announced Billy proudly, setting down his pick.

Couldn't he feel it? Couldn't he feel the… She clasped her arms around herself. Couldn't he feel the malevolence that clung to this place?

His face was bright and eager; his eyes alight with excitement as he peered into the gaping black hole.

"You first or me?" he asked, and when she shrank back he picked up the flashlight and grinned.

"Me then. But you have to follow. It was your idea remember."

As Laura stepped into the inky blackness, for a mo-

ment she felt as if the breath was being sucked from her body. She clung to the back of Billy's jacket and sensing her fear, he laughed, a loud, normal burst of genuine amusement that seemed to magically evaporate the hovering tension. Suddenly she could breathe again.

"There, you see?" he told her, swinging the beam of the flashlight around the damp gray walls. "Nothing... There's nothing here."

"Can't you feel it?"

Her voice was a whisper in the darkness.

"Feel what? I can feel that it's cold and damp in here and I can certainly smell something pretty rank."

Laura's hand tightened on his jacket.

"Something evil. This place feels evil."

Billy frowned, disconcerted for a moment by the strange pitch of her voice.

"Laura! For heaven's sake, I'd better get you outside into the fresh air before your imagination runs away with you completely. Look... "

He took hold of her shoulder and slowly ran the light right around the walls of the cave again, forcing her to follow its progress.

"You see, there is nothing in here. Now do you believe me?"

The air had never smelled so sweet to Laura as they left the cave and headed back to the horses. She desperately tried to put her crazy feelings on hold, knowing Billy was right. Anything that may have lived in that cave was long gone and they would probably never know why it was walled up in the first place. She should just forget they ever came here at all.

The horses waited patiently, still securely tied to the tree, and even Toby seemed subdued. He had run off when Billy started to smash down the stones, frightened by the noise. Now he lay near their bags, curled up in a tight little ball.

"All right, lad?" murmured Billy, scooping him up and the little dog whined, pushing his cold nose into the crook of his master's neck.

"Something has certainly spooked him," remarked Billy, and an icy shiver rippled down Laura's spine.

"Let's go home," she begged.

"Now that we've laid your ghost to rest?" he laughed, swinging into the saddle with Toby still in his arms.

"Have we?" she whispered.

Chapter Six

Sam Whitmore slowed the car to a halt, wrenched on the hand brake and looked around at his wife and daughter with a puzzled frown.

"Are you sure we're on the right road? You told me that it was only two miles from the village. Maybe we've passed it."

"Mr. Flynne told me to turn left at the church and just keep on going," announced Rachel. "Go a bit farther."

With a resigned sigh Sam put the car into gear and released the clutch to pull slowly out into the lane again, and as they rounded the next corner, Penny gave a squeal of excitement.

"I can see it," she cried. "Look… there's the sign."

"*Hightor. Horses Of Distinction,*" read out Rachel. "Well, it certainly sounds impressive."

"We'll see," retorted her husband dryly. "I've heard that some of these horse dealers can be pretty unscrupulous."

"Well, Mr. Flynne comes with the very best recommendations," announced Rachel, as the car pulled up into the yard and stopped next to a large blue horse-box. "Look how neat and tidy everything is."

Several well-groomed equine heads stared out inquisitively over freshly-painted stable doors. Not a wisp of hay or straw marked the perfectly swept tarmac surface. Brightly painted tubs containing a variety of evergreen bushes made attractive splashes of color against the gray stone walls.

"That is certainly true," remarked Sam, his expression brightening at the orderliness of the place. "Come on, there's the office over there. Let's go and find your Mr. Flynne."

While her parents went off toward the door marked, "Office", Penny wandered across to see the horses. Her heartbeat quickened as she breathed in the scent of them, gently stroking each warm, smooth nose as she tried to guess which one they intended for her. Grays, chestnuts and bays, thoroughbreds and stocky cobs, they were all so different, and yet all so wonderful. Which one would suit her best? She didn't really have a clue – except for Storm of course. But she knew that he would always have to remain a painted dream. And then, incredibly, the dream came true.

From the moment she saw the beautiful black horse come prancing around the corner of the barn, Penny knew that it was Storm. Time seemed to stand still and her whole body tingled as she stared at him, absorbing his familiar form with a kind of dreamlike wonder. She had stood gazing at him in the painting so many times, but now, seeing him in the flesh left her breathless.

But how could it be Storm? That was impossible, wasn't it? Wild ideas ran through her head, perhaps the painting wasn't really old at all…

Totally mesmerized, she barely noticed the elderly man who was leading him, so when he spoke to her she just stared at him vacantly for a moment.

"Are you all right, lass?" he repeated, bringing his charge to a reluctant halt. The gleaming black gelding spun round in a circle and then stopped, staring toward the horizon, his nostrils flaring as he raised his head and snorted loudly.

"Sorry," she began. "Yes I… What do you call this horse?"

Her voice held a kind of wonder and he gave her a curious glance before replying.

"Aladdin. He's called Aladdin. Now what can I help you with, miss? Are you looking for Mike Flynne?"

She took a step toward him, hand outstretched and heart pounding like a drum inside her chest. It must be Storm. It had to be. Even the expression in his huge dark eyes was the same – kind of wild and distant – as if he could see something no one else could. And yet she knew in her heart of hearts that it wasn't possible. Where was her mother? She would know.

"Here's Mike now," announced the old man, with obvious relief. Penny dragged her eyes away from the beautiful black horse to see her parents walking toward them accompanied by a broad, stockily built man. She presumed he must be Mike Flynne.

She held her breath, watching eagerly for her mother's reaction and when Rachel saw Aladdin – standing motionless now, his whole body taut and quivering – the color drained from her face. She stopped in her tracks.

"It is Storm, Mom… isn't it? cried Penny. "It *has* to be him."

Rachel shook her head slowly with disbelief.

"Well, I must admit it gave me a shock to see him standing there, but I am afraid that the Storm in our painting is over two hundred years old. This fellow certainly doesn't look as old as that… He is the spitting image of him, though, I'll give you that."

Noting Rachel's interest in Aladdin, Mike Flynne pushed his hat back on his head and stepped forward to get her attention.

"Sorry to disappoint you Mrs. Whitmore, but I'm afraid that this one isn't for sale."

Penny's heart plummeted as she felt her dreams collapsing, but her mother looked around with a smile.

"Oh I think he would be far too much horse and a bit too much money for us at the moment Mr. Flynne," she said. Sensing her daughter's disappointment she took hold of her arm.

"Mr. Flynne says he has a horse that would be much more suitable for you, darling," she told her, following her gaze once again toward the beautiful black gelding.

"It can't really be Storm you know," she added in an undertone and Penny nodded.

"It was just a shock at first, you know... seeing him standing there when we have spent so much time talking about him."

"Talking about Storm," insisted Rachel. "Not this horse."

"Aladdin here belongs to a young friend of mine," interrupted Mike. "She must be about the same age as you, I'll have to introduce you. If you buy a horse, I'm sure she'd be happy to give you a hand with it." Then he grinned. "When she's not working for me or at school, of course. Now I'll just have a word with Jim, here, and then we'll go and see the cob."

He caught up with the old groom just as he was about to take Aladdin into his stable.

"Is he all right?" he asked. "Why have you brought him in?

Jim shrugged.

"He was galloping round the field like a demented idiot. Something has spooked him. I don't know what's the matter with the horse at the moment."

Mike frowned.

"Well the lass should be back soon... and that son of mine. He promised to be here for 3 o'clock."

Jim's mouth twisted into a smile.

"He still has five minutes," he remarked, as they heard the sound of hooves, clattering down the lane.

By the time they arrived back at Hightor Laura had almost convinced herself that Billy was right. The cave was empty. She had seen that with her own eyes, and the weird feelings of something evil and very scary were just her own wild imagination.

"You should write a book," Billy had laughingly suggested when she tried to tell him how she felt, and then he had trotted on ahead off her, more worried about being late than listening to her crazy ideas. There was nothing in the cave and that was good enough for him. By the time she reached Hightor Laura thought it was good enough for her, too.

The first person she saw when she jumped lightly down from the saddle was old Jim. He came hurrying toward them with an expression of concern on his weather-worn face and she immediately tensed.

"That horse of yours has led me a right merry dance," he exclaimed. "And Billy, you'd better get yourself over to the office. The Whitmore's are here to see the cob."

With an impudent grin, Billy held his watch aloft.

"Dead on three Jim… Look. I'm bang on time."

"Tell that to your dad," smiled Jim. "Now give me your horse and get yourself gone."

Billy whistled as he walked away, his strides easy and relaxed and Jim shook his head in despair as he ran up the chestnut's stirrups.

"Never takes anything seriously," he remarked, and Laura shrugged.

"You know Billy. But never mind him. What about Aladdin?"

Jim took the horse's reins over its head before replying and they fell in together side by side, their charges following willingly.

"I don't know what has gotten into him," he told her. "There's something spooking him. After you two left he just kept on galloping around the field, so I brought him in."

"And how is he now?"

At the expression on Laura's face the old man smiled.

"Now come on, lass, don't go worrying yourself. Something has got him a bit stressed, that's all. You will have these highly-strung Arabs; should have bought yourself a horse like Cuthbert, here."

Laura patted the chestnut's solid neck.

"Since when has he been called Cuthbert," she laughed.

"Since I decided that it suited him," Jim told her. "Now get him sorted out and go and see to your crazy Arab."

When Penny saw the two chestnuts come into the yard she felt a rush of shy excitement, watching eagerly while the boy and girl dismounted. Could the boy from Faversham Wood really be Mike Flynne's son?

The girl went off with the horses, but he strode easily toward them accompanied by Toby. When the little dog ran across to greet her, Penny bent down hurriedly, hiding her confusion in its soft black coat.

"You are late," snapped Mike Flynne, but the boy

simply flashed him the same disarming smile that Penny had seen on their previous acquaintance.

"Oh no I'm not," he declared, pointing at his watch. "Three o clock, you said."

Mike Flynne mumbled something unintelligible in response, then swung his hand wide and looked at her parents.

"Meet my son," he announced. "Billy, this is Mr. and Mrs. Whitway and their daughter… "

"We've already met," murmured Billy, staring straight into Penny's eyes as she rose to her feet.

"Penny… my name… it's Penny," she stuttered, staring at the ground, and to her relief Mike Flynne ushered them all off toward the row of stables beyond the barn.

"Right then," he called. "Let's go and see this horse. Billy, you get his tack and I'll fetch him out."

Penny may have still secretly clung to the hope that her horse might look like Storm's double, but she took to Cheerful's lovely kind expression at once. As Mike Flynne led him out into the yard the mist lifted and the sun broke through the clouds, turning his rich bay coat to mahogany as he stood motionless, a handsome picture of dependability.

She walked eagerly toward him and when he looked straight at her with shining brown eyes, nickering gently, her mouth widened into a broad smile and she patted his neck enthusiastically.

"He's lovely… isn't he?" She exclaimed, looking at her mother.

Rachel nodded in agreement and turned toward Mike Flynne.

"Can she have a ride on him please?"

"Do what you want with him," said Mike. "Billy will ride him for you first, though."

When Billy mounted up, Cheerful arched his neck and trotted willingly forward with big, ground-covering strides.

"There you go," announced Mike Flynne enthusiastically. "Safe as a house."

Penny clutched her mother's sleeve with excitement.

"Isn't he brilliant?" she whispered.

Rachel smiled.

"As brilliant as Storm, or that Aladdin?" she asked.

"As brilliant in a different way," Penny told her. "Can I ride him?"

"Well that's what you came for," remarked Mike Flynne, overhearing her.

Billy brought the cob to a halt and Penny walked toward him, suddenly uncertain.

"I'm not very good you know," she admitted.

"Every one has to start somewhere," came another voice. Penny looked at its owner and met the gray eyes of the girl from the forest.

"I'm Laura," she said, with a friendly smile. "And don't worry, Cheerful will look after you."

At first Penny had trouble with her rising trot, but the cob's paces were so comfortable and he was so eager to please, that after a few minutes they were moving around the school in perfect harmony.

Eventually she pulled him up and leaned down to pat his neck, her whole face shining with enthusiasm.

"Can we buy him, Dad… please," she begged.

Rachel Whitway looked at her husband appealingly and he raised his eyes skywards.

"Okay, Mr. Flynne," he asked. "How much?"

"Please… call me Mike," was the reply. "And if you come to my office I'll get you a drink and we'll talk business."

A tingle of excitement rippled throughout Penny's whole body and her toes curled up inside her boots. Storm, or Aladdin, would always be her dream horse, but Cheerful was real.

"Jump down," suggested Billy. "And we'll put him away.

While he ran up the stirrups and loosened the girth, Penny stood mesmerized, just staring at Cheerful. He pricked his ears toward her, nuzzling her arm as though he knew that she was about to become his new mistress. There was a kind expression on his lovely face and his whole demeanor oozed a dependability that made her feel happy and safe and just so lucky to have found him.

"I think he is going to be my best friend," she exclaimed, and Laura smiled.

"Maybe we can all be friends," she suggested. After all, we don't live so far away. And I can give you a hand with him… if you want me to that is."

"Thanks," responded Penny. "I think I'll need all the help I can get."

"Well let's hope that your parents and my dad can agree on a price, then," remarked Billy, handing Cheerful's reins to Laura. "Can you see to him please, I promised to go and help Jim with the three year old." He turned toward Penny.

"And I will see you soon I'm sure... Green Eyes."

"I hope so," she replied.

Laura was pleased that the girl from Faversham Wood was going to buy Cheerful. She seemed like someone who would really love him, and Cheerful deserved that.

"Come on," she said. "Let's put him away."

By the time they had untacked, brushed him off, and tied up a haynet, the two girls were already chattering away like old friends.

"I can't bear to leave him," sighed Penny as they closed the stable door behind them and she leaned over it to look at him one last time.

Laura smiled understandingly.

"I know what you mean. I don't know what I would do without my horse."

"He looks super," agreed Penny. "I love chestnuts."

Laura frowned then her face lightened.

"Oh!" she laughed. "Cuthbert isn't mine, I was just exercising him. My horse is over here."

She led the way to the row of stables beside the barn and when Penny peered eagerly over the half door, for a moment it seemed that time stood still as she stared once again into the wild black eyes of the horse from the painting.

"Storm," she breathed.

"No... Aladdin," Laura told her with a puzzled smile. "His name is Aladdin."

The black gelding stood quivering at the back of its box, head held high and nostrils flared. Penny closed her eyes for a moment, feeling the fear that flooded from the lovely animal.

"Are you all right?"

Laura's tentative question brought her straight back to her senses and she dragged her eyes away from him.

"Sorry, It's just... well... I have seen him before, or at least his double. It gave me a surprise that's all."

"Aladdin has a double?"

Before Laura could ask any more the Whitways appeared in the yard, accompanied by a beaming Mike Flynne. Rachel rushed over to her daughter, arms outstretched.

"You now have your own horse," she cried, dancing her around in a circle. "He's being delivered tomorrow."

In all the excitement that followed Laura couldn't find space to question Penny again about Aladdin's double, and long after they had left she still stood staring at him.

"What is it, boy?" she asked him gently. "What has upset you so much?"

His response was to move to the doorway again, staring at the skyline as though seeing something everyone else couldn't. She ran her hand down his neck.

"Don't worry, boy," she told him. "I'll look after you."

Tomorrow, she decided, she would ask Mike if she could go with them to deliver Cheerful. Something told her that she needed to know more about the horse that looked like Aladdin.

Chapter Seven

It was dusk by the time Laura left for home and she sang as she walked along the lane. All her fears about the cave seemed very far away now. Billy had laughed at what he called her crazy ideas when she tried to talk to him again, making her feel a bit embarrassed, and everything had slipped neatly back into perspective. Even Aladdin seemed to have overcome his nerves. She had left him tucking into his evening feed enthusiastically without even a glimmer of stress.

"It must have been a touch of colic," Mike had remarked when he did his usual evening rounds. The tiny, apprehensive butterfly, that had been fluttering around in her rib cage all day, flickered and died, leaving behind a kind of relieved contentment.

Long shadows fell across the road ahead of her and the trees made dark shapes against the graying sky, but Laura didn't even notice. She had walked the short distance from Hightor to Cherry Tree Cottage so many times now that its familiarity made her feel quite safe, even as darkness fell. She was quite comfortable with the strange, distant, echoing sounds of the night.

Tomorrow Cheerful was going to his new home; now there was nice thing that had happened today. She liked the idea of helping Penny with him and it would be great to have a friend – someone to ride with. Of course she had Billy, but he was different, he was... just Billy.

After supper she slumped into a chair in front of the TV, ignoring all her mother's remarks about catching up with homework.

"We're off school this week, remember," she cried, and her mother shook her head in despair.

"Well, do some of it tomorrow night then," she insisted. "Don't forget that you have exams coming up after Christmas."

"I won't need any exams if I'm going to work with horses when I leave school," remarked Laura with a cheeky grin. Her mother frowned.

"We'll just see about that, my girl. Anyway, you need exams whatever line of work you're going into."

It was such a normal evening that she never even thought about her nightmare as she snuggled into bed; not until her heavy eyelids began to droop and by then it was too late.

Something yowled in the darkness and she felt the suffocating fear burning her lungs as the great black horse beneath her tensed itself for flight. Blackness enveloped them, a deep, dark blackness that was so much more than just the shadow of the night, and she wrapped her legs around Aladdin's heaving sides. But it wasn't Aladdin. It was Storm. It was Storm who leaped forward into the darkness, crashing blindly through the trees to escape the evil that snapped and snarled at their heels.

Laura clung to the horse's streaming mane as he increased his pace, leaning forward over his neck, all the time knowing, with a deep inner certainty, that they could never escape.

The fear was like a living thing, consuming her, and yet beneath it she felt such a terrible sadness and sense of loss that even the fear was overcome… until she saw the gaping chasm that loomed ahead and felt the yowling evil strike.

She awoke shivering, yet damp with sweat. The dream was fresh in her mind, its terror and sadness so horribly real that she jumped out of bed and switched on the light. Her room was the same. She had expected change but everything was comfortably familiar and so normal that her racing heart began to slow down. It was just a dream, just a harmless dream.

But who was Storm? And then she remembered Penny Whitway's reaction when she had seen Aladdin. She had called him Storm. That must be what had triggered the nightmare – that and her deep-rooted worries about Aladdin's unsettled behavior. She must persuade Mike Flynne to let her go with them to deliver

Cheerful, and then she could ask Penny about this horse, Storm.

No matter how much she tried to tell herself that nightmares weren't real, the fear still lingered in the back of her mind. She couldn't seem to get rid of the terrible feeling of sadness she had experienced in the dream. She tossed and turned, trying to think of anything else. Eventually, giving up on sleep, she crept out of bed before dawn, dressed hurriedly, and tiptoed down the stairs.

The kitchen was warm but she didn't dare linger to savor its comfort in case her parents woke, so she just grabbed her jacket and a bag of potato chips before stepping out onto the porch to push her feet into the cold depths of her rubber boots. Then she jogged down the lane, keeping her mind firmly set on the day ahead.

Hightor was still in darkness when she opened the yard gates and she walked quickly across to flick the switch at the end of the long stable block, bathing the whole area in a warm yellow glow. Horses' heads appeared over their half doors, eyes shining in the glare of electric light. She walked uneasily toward the empty space above Aladdin's door. He was usually the most inquisitive horse on the yard.

Her heart sank when she saw him standing at the back of his box.

"Hey, boy," she whispered. "I'm here now. What is it?"

He raised his head, neck arched, blowing softly through his nostrils.

"It's only me, boy," she murmured, opening the door and as she stared into the fathomless depth of his gleaming dark eyes, for one brief moment the weirdest, most ridiculous feeling came over her that she was looking into the eyes of a stranger. She shivered and reached out her hand as if in protest, then he nickered urgently and recognition dawned. Was she going totally insane?

"Laura Taylor. Whatever are you doing here at this time of the morning? Couldn't you sleep?"

Mike Flynne's loud jarring tones brought normality flooding back, and she looked at him with a welcoming smile.

"I was worried about Aladdin. He still seems to be a bit stressed out or scared or something."

Mike stepped into the stable.

"I told you he might have had a touch of colic... and look. He's cut himself."

Laura's eyes flew to where Mike was studying Aladdin's flank.

"Now don't you go getting yourself all worried about it," He insisted. "Its just a few scratches. Jim will put some of his magical ointment on them and they'll be gone in no time. You'll see."

He traced the three lines with his forefinger as if to convince himself.

"Yes... just superficial. Better have a good look around his box, though, to see if there is a sharp nail or something. And don't worry about the colic. If it were anything serious he'd be doing a whole lot more than just looking a bit tense and having the odd roll. Now come on, settle him down and let's get some work done. We have a horse to deliver today, remember."

When he had gone Laura took another look at Aladdin's wounds. They stretched right down his flank in three lines, like scratch marks.

"What could you have been doing, boy?" she murmured and when he pushed his face against her, wanting attention, she placed her arm around his neck wondering what could have made her think he seemed unfamiliar.

"Don't you worry, Aladdin," she told him. "I won't let anything happen to you."

Over breakfast they all discussed Aladdin's injuries.

"No good having a horse at all if you get upset every time it has a bit of a cut or a touch of colic," remarked Jim dryly. "Specially if you happen to own a crazy, highly-strung Arab."

"He's worth the extra effort," laughed Laura and the old man shook his head.

"You should be buying Cheerful," he grumbled. "Now there's a proper horse."

Mike Flynne, who had been sitting in silence with a thoughtful expression on his face, stood up then and walked across to warm his backside by the stove.

"Speaking of Cheerful," he said, "we have a bit of a problem there. I have a client looking for a horse to show jump and he wants to call in here around lunchtime. He's a good client, and I have a few horses that might suit him. The thing is, I need Billy to show them off for me and Jim will have to see to the dentist. He's coming at 1 o'clock to take a wolf tooth out of the stallion, and he may as well check some of the others while he's here; there must be a few that need rasping."

Billy looked up from his breakfast, laden fork poised halfway between the plate and his mouth.

"Okay, Dad we get your drift. Why don't you just come out with it?"

"Well…"

Mike pushed his fingers into his graying thatch of curls and scratched the back of his head.

"I thought maybe the lass, here, might like to ride Cheerful over to the Whitways for me. It's not that far and she could take a shortcut through the wood – there's a gate that leads directly from the pathway into the garden of Faversham Hall. Mrs. Whitway suggested it when I rang to tell her that I might not be able to get there until tomorrow. She thought it would be nice if Laura could stay for a bit, to help her daughter settle the cob in."

"Oh, so you've already arranged it then?" remarked Billy, looking around at Laura. "You don't have to go if you don't want to."

"Oh no. I don't mind … honestly. I'd like to go."

As soon as the words left her lips Laura realized that they were true. She did want to go to Faversham Hall with Cheerful and get to know Penny

Whitmore... Apart from the bit about Faversham Wood, that is. The very thought of going there alone after last time left a horrible feeling of dread in the pit of her stomach, but she certainly wasn't going to let it stop her.

"I'll just exercise Aladdin and then I'll get the cob ready," she said with a smile. "But you'll have to give me good directions."

"And take a mobile phone with you," added Jenny Flynne as she leaned over to fill the toaster.

"For sure," exclaimed Billy. "You can use mine. It'll be worth going without it to save me having to search the whole wood for you again."

Laura pushed back the prickle of alarm that made her scalp tingle.

"Don't worry," she told him in a very definite tone. "There's no way I'll get lost this time, and I can't see Cheerful bolting off in fright can you?"

Billy grinned.

"Guess not," he agreed. Then for just a moment his voice took on a serious note.

"Be careful, though, stay on the path and ring if there's any problem."

"I might go looking for the cave," teased Laura and he laughed out loud.

"Absolutely no chance."

Laura was relieved to find that Aladdin seemed much calmer when she went through the familiar motions of grooming and tacking up. He nuzzled her as she carefully brushed his face and she fed him a piece of carrot, remembering her ridiculous feeling early that morning, the weird sensation that it wasn't Aladdin looking back at her. It must have been the horrible nightmare that had made her over-imaginative.

Something quivered deep inside her chest and she put all her efforts into wielding the body brush and curry comb, concentrating fiercely to try and push away the images from the dream. It was just a dream after all.

When she reached his flank she gently traced the scratches with her fingers. They were drying up already, just as Mike Flynne had said they would, but she still didn't know what caused them in the first place. She and Billy had both searched the whole box, but there didn't seem to be anything that could have caused an injury.

"Just one of those things," Mike had announced with a shrug. "That's horses for you. You never know what they are going to do next."

Aladdin seemed excited as Laura led him out into the yard and when she mounted up in the outdoor school, he leaped eagerly forward, prancing and sidling toward the gate. She closed her hands firmly on the reins, trying hopelessly to get him to settle into walk, but he just kept on breaking into a trot and napping toward the entrance. With an exasperated sigh, she pushed him on into working trot and rode around in endless, hopeless circles, desperately trying to cling to the patience that normally didn't desert her.

Mike Flynne passed by, leading one of his show jumping hopefuls in from the field, and he stopped for a moment to watch her progress.

"He still looks a bit tense," he remarked with a frown.

Laura sighed and brought her unwilling mount back to walk, glad of an excuse to stop.

"I don't know what it is," she cried. "Our schooling has been going so well, but now he just keeps heading toward the gate and he won't even settle into a decent trot. I've never known him to be such a complete pain."

"Well, I wouldn't do too much with him if he's still not feeling right," advised Mike. "Give him the benefit of the doubt. Why don't you turn him out in the far field before you go? I'll get Billy to bring him in for you this afternoon. That'll do him more good than anything. You can't beat a bit of Dr. Green."

Guilt flooded through Laura at the relief she felt. Never before had she been so frustrated with her precious horse, even in the early stages when he was a quivering wreck.

"Thanks," she told Mike. "I'll put him out now and then head out to Faversham Hall."

Mike gave her a wide grin then clicked at his charge from under his tongue and led it off toward the stables.

"I'll be in the office when you're ready to go," he called as an afterthought. "Best make sure we get the directions right."

As soon as she jumped down Aladdin seemed to settle, which did nothing to relieve her guilt. When she turned him out he stood as still as a statue, gazing toward the horizon with a far-away look in his eyes.

"Okay, boy," she called, and just for a moment he looked toward her before trotting off across the grass, tail raised like a banner behind him.

Cheerful felt oddly wide after Aladdin, as Laura trotted him along the lane. His thick neck stretched out in front of her gave a comforting feel of solidity. She couldn't imagine anything daunting the easy going cob and that thought lent her confidence as they approached the entrance to Faversham Wood.

The latch on the gate stuck, and as she struggled to release it, Cheerful took the opportunity to dive down for a snack. By the time she had negotiated the narrow entrance and regained control of her greedy mount, they were inside Faversham Wood without her even thinking about it.

"Come on, boy," she said out loud, patting him firmly on the neck.

Her voice echoed in the hollow silence, and when she urged Cheerful into trot along the pathway, his hooves thudded softly in her ears. She didn't notice the dark shape that slunk through the undergrowth as the gate clicked shut behind her. Didn't see the glowing amber eyes that followed her progress through the trees.

Chapter Eight

Penny Whitway woke up with a knot in the bottom of her stomach. Today was the day her horse was being delivered and she had never felt so excited about anything in her entire life.

The day dragged. She had redone Cheerful's stable a dozen times and now stood staring at the smooth expanse of carefully arranged straw, the banks neatly rolled into such perfect curves that they were nothing less than a masterpiece.

"Fit for Storm himself," announced her mother from behind her, and Penny looked around eagerly, her face bright with anticipation.

"Have they phoned?"

"Five minutes ago. It will take Laura about half an hour to get here so you've just got time to… "

Before her mother had even finished her sentence, Penny was walking away across the garden. Rachel laughed.

"Oh well," she called after her. "I suppose you are too excited to eat, anyway."

"Sorry," mouthed Penny, turning to look back, then she headed off again, determined not to miss Laura's approach.

The gate creaked on its hinges as she pushed it open and she paused, waiting for her usual apprehension about the forest to kick in, but it wasn't there.

Way overhead the trees loomed toward the distant, moving patchwork of gray sky. Ahead of her the pathway stretched through the undergrowth like a smooth brown ribbon, a ribbon along which, at any moment, Cheerful might appear.

She sank down onto a fallen log, listening for the sound of his approach, her eyes bright with such excitement that even Faversham Wood had lost its mystery.

The minutes ticked by. She watched a beetle make careful progress across the mossy log and saw a gray squirrel jump through the trees above her head. Then at last she heard a distant thudding sound. She jumped to her feet as the sound came closer and alarm bells began to ring.

The thud was turning into thunder, the thunder of galloping hooves. Surely Laura wouldn't be galloping so madly along the narrow track.

Anger rose and dreams of a budding friendship faded as she realized that the opinion she had formed of Laura must be completely wrong. She obviously wasn't even a real horse lover.

She could see Cheerful now, his chunky, mahogany-colored body charging toward her at full tilt, his nostrils extended to show a flash of red and his coat matted with sweat.

His rider leaned low on his neck; her legs – even now when they were almost here – beat a crazy tattoo on his sides and her face… Penny shivered when she saw Laura's expression, and all her anger faded… Her face was a mask of pure terror.

Cheerful stumbled to a halt in front of her and Penny grabbed his rein and dragged him through the gate into the safety of the garden.

"What is it?" she cried. "What has happened?"

For a moment Laura couldn't speak. She just lay on Cheerful's neck while he stood stock still, his sides heaving and his breath coming in deep, heavy pants.

"Sorry," she eventually mumbled. "I'm so sorry."

"Never mind that."

Penny grabbed her arm to help her slide to the ground.

"Just tell me what happened."

For a moment Laura was silent and then she took a deep breath and tried to smile.

"Look," she said. "This is your day and I am not going to spoil it… Anyway you'd never believe me."

"Try me."

At the concern in Penny's voice, Laura's eyes filled up and she turned away.

"We'll get Cheerful settled first," she said. "Then we'll see."

"No."

Penny stood her ground.

"Something has obviously frightened you witless and you've got to tell me what it was."

Laura's whole body shuddered and she clasped her hands across her face as the fear flooded back.

"It was just after I got through the gate. Cheerful was trotting along so happily and I… "

She hesitated, unsure if she should go on, but when Penny squeezed her arm she took a great deep breath.

"I know that this sounds ridiculous but… I felt the evil, you see. The evil from before, from the cave. It was all around me, suffocating me. And then… and then I saw a movement in the bushes and I just knew that it had come to get me. It was like the dream. It was just like being in the dream, but it was real and I had to get away…

As her voice petered out, for just a moment an image flashed into Penny's mind, the image of Laura in the forest, cantering off after Billy and behind her… She closed her eyes, trying not to think about the dark shape she had seen in the forest that day.

"You think I'm crazy don't you?"

Laura's voice was little more than a whisper and there was a kind of desperation in her eyes.

"No," said Penny, knowing it was true. "No, I don't think you're crazy and I don't know what you mean about the evil or the dream… but I do believe that something strange is going on. I think it's linked to the wood."

For Laura it was like a huge weight being lifted from her shoulders. She was no longer alone with her fear and her wild imagination.

"Thanks for believing in me," she said, her voice choked with emotion and she felt a kind of strength seeping back into her bones.

"Come on, then," suggested Penny with a broad grin. "Let's go and get my new horse settled, and then you can tell me everything."

"Right from the beginning?" asked Laura.

"Right from the beginning," she repeated firmly.

Totally unconcerned by the episode in the woods, Cheerful tucked happily into his haynet. Together the girls had cooled him off and brushed him down until his mahogany coat gleamed. By tacit agreement neither of them mentioned the thing that lingered in the back of their minds like a dark cloud, until at last Penny put down her brush.

"All right," she announced. "I'll get us a drink and then you can start."

They sat on a hay bale; sipping cans of soda and nibbling on the biscuits that Rachel Whitway had just taken from the oven. It seemed a million miles away from caves and dreams and horses that weren't themselves. So much so, in fact, that Laura began to doubt herself.

"Go on," urged Penny, noticing her hesitation. "You'll have to tell me now. Just start right at the beginning, when you first got Aladdin and then I want to know every detail of everything that has happened since, even if it doesn't seem that important."

For Laura it was like opening a floodgate and as she calmly delivered her story, beginning with her move, and the day she first saw Aladdin, and ending with her mad gallop through Faversham Wood that very morning. Penny felt the hairs on the back of her neck rise and the first tendrils of fear rippled down her spine. A frozen silence fell between them when Laura finished. For several seconds Laura watched Penny's reaction as her words sank in, then she put on a forcedly cheerful face and tried to smile.

"So," she said, "Now I suppose you really do think I'm completely insane."

Penny just looked at her for a moment then she slowly stood up and beckoned her to follow.

"Here… "

She spoke quite softly but there was a deep urgency to her tone.

"I want to show you something."

Neither of the girls said another word as they went into the house through the huge, old-fashioned kitchen and walked hurriedly along a corridor. It opened into a bright, sunny, square-shaped hallway with several oak doors leading off it. Penny opened the nearest one and ushered Laura inside. The room was spacious and bright with light from the tall windows that graced two sides. It had an antique dining table in the center, and a large bowl of vibrant cuttings made a splash of color against the pale yellow of the walls. Laura thought she had never seen such a lovely room, but as she gazed around in admiration Penny took hold of her arm.

"There," she announced, pointing at the painting above the fireplace.

When Laura saw the beautiful black horse that stood forever staring at the distant horizon, she froze, unable to deal with the emotion that flooded through her. This time it was Penny who waited quietly and watched *her* reaction, knowing exactly how she felt.

"Who is it?" Laura eventually asked, her voice little more than a whisper.

"She is the last Lady Faversham," announced Penny proudly. "And she once lived in this very house."

"And that is your Storm," breathed Laura.

"Or your Aladdin," finished Penny.

Laura's face blanched.

"It is Aladdin," she cried. "The Aladdin I saw in the stable this morning." Then she fiercely grabbed hold of Penny's arm.

"What is going on?"

For a moment the two girls simply stared at each other until Penny broke the strained silence.

"I don't really believe in ghosts or demons," she said, her voice filled with a kind of amused disbelief. "But I do know that there is something really weird going on around here. I mean, things like this just don't happen to ordinary people like us, do they?"

With a burst of confidence inspired by Penny's support Laura grinned.

"It seems that they do now, so we'll just have to get to the bottom of it."

"And I know how. At least I know how to make a

start," burst out Penny. "The last Lady Faversham and her horse, Storm, met a terrible end and I think it has something to do with Faversham Wood being haunted. My mother has a book. Dad bought it for her. It's about lore and legends around here..."

"And you think the book might give us a clue?"

Penny shrugged.

"Who knows? It's worth a try."

An enticing aroma drifted through the doorway as they burst into the large, airy kitchen, intent upon looking for the book. Rachel Whitway was stirring something on the old stove and she looked around with a smile, her pleasant face pink from the heat.

"All right you two," she insisted. "I've made you some nice soup for lunch, so sit yourselves down and I'll serve it up."

Laura looked helplessly at the large steaming bowl in front of her; the last thing she felt like doing was eating. She took a spoonful, sipping slowly. Before she knew it, the bowl was empty and she was on her second hunk of freshly baked bread.

Penny had been very quiet as they ate; so quiet in fact, that her mother kept giving her a worried look.

"Everything all right with Cheerful?" she eventually asked, and Penny's face lit up.

"He's wonderful," she cried, "and Laura has been a real help."

"I'm glad you two are getting along," smiled Rachel. "Are you going to ride him after lunch?"

"Of course," replied Penny. "Oh, and by the way, Mom, do you think we could have a look at your book? I've been showing Laura the painting."

Laura's spoon clattered into her empty bowl and she felt something tighten in her stomach as she waited for the reply.

"Of course you can, but you'll have to wait until your father comes home. He's taken it to work with him; one of his colleagues is interested in that sort of thing."

Rachel started collecting the dishes then, completely unaware of how her words were affecting the two girls and they stood up simultaneously.

"Have you looked at it yet?" asked Penny, and her mother paused for a moment.

"I've given it a quick glance," she replied. "And I did find a bit about Lady Faversham, but I haven't had the chance to read it through thoroughly. It's quite spooky. Something to do with a black witch."

"Do you know any more?"

Rachel frowned at the intensity in her daughter's voice.

"No not really. Anyway, your dad should be back by 6 o'clock so you can read it for yourself. I'll call him at work and remind him not to forget it."

The two girls walked slowly across the grass toward Cheerful's stable.

"Now what?" asked Penny.

"Now," replied Laura very definitely. "We tack up

Cheerful and I give you some helpful advice on how to ride him. I mean, if you think about it nothing has actually happened has it? Apart from me having horrible nightmares and being scared out of my wits by the weird feelings, and all."

"But what about Aladdin? What about the way he is behaving?" asked in Penny.

For a moment Laura went quiet, then she gave a determined kind of grin.

"Maybe he really has had colic and my imagination has been running away with me again."

Penny's forehead puckered into a slight frown and she nodded.

"Well let's hope that is all it is," she said. "But tonight I'll still read the book and find out what I can. If it's of any help I'll phone you."

"Or better still," suggested Laura. "Ride Cheerful over to Hightor first thing in the morning and we'll look at it together."

"I'd better get some serious practice in then," laughed Penny. "There is one slight problem with that, though. To get to Hightor I have to ride through the woods."

The horrified expression on Laura's face brought an amused glint in her eyes.

"Don't worry," she insisted. "Whatever it is – if it is anything at all – I don't think it's interested in me. I'll go and get the tack, and you can help me put it on."

Cheerful was so obliging that Penny was soon trotting and cantering him around the small paddock at the bottom of the garden with such confidence that she couldn't help giving a whoop of delight, and as she watched, Laura felt her fears fading. Her panic attack in the wood seemed a million miles away and the comments she had made to Penny became more and more feasible by the minute.

In fact, by the time her new-found friend reined in and jumped down to fling her arms around her chunky mount's thick neck, Laura had discovered a whole new confidence that carried her through the rest of the afternoon and stayed with her right until the moment when she came face to face with Aladdin again.

Chapter Nine

When a small red car pulled up in the entrance to Hightor, Billy Flynne was trudging across the yard with a feed bucket in each hand, his shoulders hunched against the steady drizzle that had just begun. He stopped to see who it was and a broad smile spread across his face when he saw Laura climbing out of it.

"You took your time," he called, placing the buckets down onto the tarmac.

The car swung around and she waved at the driver as it sped off down the lane again before turning toward him with a cheeky grin.

"Only following your dad's orders. Have to keep his clients happy you know. Oh, and by the way, here's your phone. I didn't need it after all, but thanks anyway."

"Obviously everything went well then," he remarked as she fumbled in her pocket and Laura's face lit up.

"Better than that. In fact it was brilliant… Now where did I put the thing? Ah, here it is."

As she pulled out the phone and handed it over to Billy, just for a fleeting moment she caught his eye, and there was something about his expression that brought back the slight prickle of alarm that hovered relentlessly, awaiting its moment.

"Is something wrong?"

Billy shrugged and averted his eyes.

"It's Aladdin isn't it? Is he all right?"

He frowned and a band tightened around her chest.

"It depends what you mean by all right."

His voice was cautious, unrevealing.

"I mean, well he looks fine, but we had to bring him in from the field again before he did himself some harm. He just seems upset… you know… not himself."

"Not himself."

The words echoed inside her head as she walking quickly toward his stable.

"Now don't go getting all paranoid on me," insisted Billy, running along behind her, buckets forgotten. "He really is okay… You'll see," he finished lamely as she peered over the stable door.

Aladdin was standing at the back of his box. His eyes held the distant expression she had seen before and his nostrils were flared, revealing a glimpse of red. When she stepped in through the door he completely ignored her.

"See," repeated Billy. "There really is nothing wrong with him, he's just had a bit of a brainstorm that's all. Now I'm going to finish feeding up."

Laura gave him a vague smile, but her heart was hammering. All she could see was Storm. The Storm from the painting… and that was insane… wasn't it?

She walked toward him making the special deep clucking sound that she always kept just for him. When she touched his neck the muscles were hard beneath her hand and he turned his head away from her, staring out over the door.

"Aladdin," she whispered. "Aladdin it's me," then she took hold of his nose and turned his face toward her, staring into his eyes and murmuring to him in the silly voice she always used when no one was listening. He snorted at her as if she were a stranger and her tone took on a more serious, desperate note.

"Aladdin where are you?" she begged. "Come back to me… please come back. Aladdin!"

For a moment he shied away from her, pulling back, but she held onto him, willing him to respond. Then quite suddenly, as if she really had touched some inner response button, the wildness within him simply seemed to fade away.

Familiarity flooded back. His huge brown eyes softened and he lowered his head, pushing his face against her chest and snuffling softly, needing comfort.

Laura felt the prick of tears and she pressed her cheek against the warm softness of his coat, breathing in his scent with a rush of guilt at her impatience of the morning. She should have followed her instincts. Something strange was happening to Aladdin and she had to help him.

"Don't worry, boy," she whispered. "I'll make it all right."

She hardly dared even allow herself to dwell upon the crazy ideas that kept coming into her head. She just knew that something very weird was going on and no one would believe her… except for Penny, she remembered with a surge of relief. At least now she had Penny. An idea began to form in the back of her mind, a way to keep an eye on Aladdin and fend off the terrifying nightmares that seemed to trigger this whole crazy business.

Once he was settled and calm and all the chores were finished, Penny rushed home. Her mother was in the bedroom changing her clothes. She came out onto the landing at the sound of her daughter's voice in the hallway below and leaned over the banister rail, her smooth blonde hair falling forward across her face.

"I'm going to my art class," she called. "Your supper is in the oven and your father should be home soon."

"Do you mind if I stay at Penny Whitway's tonight?"

There, she had said it, her plan had begun and there was no turning back now.

"Penny Whitway?"

By the way her mother pushed her hair impatiently back from her face, Laura could see that she was very late and very stressed.

"You know," she went on quickly. "From Faversham Hall. I told you about her yesterday. She's asked me to stay over. You don't need to take me, I can go on my bike."

"I'd better call her mother."

Panic set in. That would finish everything.

"For heaven's sake, Mom, I'm not ten years old you know."

Laura stood in the center of the hallway, hands firmly placed upon her hips and such an indignant expression on her face that her mother couldn't help but smile.

"All right," she reluctantly agreed, already moving back toward her bedroom. "If you really are sure that her mother doesn't mind, but call when you get there. Your father will be in."

This was going better than Laura could have expected. Now she had plenty of time to get her things together. She went into the kitchen and took a plate from the oven. Shepherds pie. The very thought of it started a sick feeling in the pit of her stomach.

Her mother's face appeared fleetingly around the door.

"Bye, darling," she called, "and don't forget to phone your father."

As soon as the front door shut, Laura placed her plate on the floor. Bounce devoured it in about three mouthfuls and looked up for more, stumpy tail wagging furiously.

"Don't be greedy," she told him as she hastily scribbled a note to her father saying she would be at Faversham Hall with Penny.

Half an hour later, clad in her warmest jacket, she was dragging her bike out from behind a stack of junk in the shed beside the cottage. Her sleeping bag was rolled in a bag that she tied to the handlebars and in her knapsack were drinks, potato chips, a flashlight, and a magazine. Behind her the kitchen lights glowed in the window and just for a moment she hesitated, looking through into the safety and comfort she was leaving behind. Doubt set in. Perhaps she should have called Penny and told her what she was doing. But no, she turned back to face the dark emptiness of the night. She had already ruined Penny's special day with her first-ever horse; this was for Aladdin. She would do it alone.

The yard at Hightor was in darkness as she stopped outside the gates. The buildings made black shadows against the deep purple of the sky and the silence was total, with not even the sound of a single horse crunching on its hay. Laura hesitated. Where should she put her bike? She looked across to where the Flynnes' house loomed beyond the barn. Even that was in darkness. They must be out. Was that good or bad? What if they came into the yard when they returned?

She took a great deep breath, realizing that panic was setting in.

"You are here at Hightor where you have been a thousand times before," she told herself. "And the Flynnes' drive is farther down the lane so they are hardly likely to come back this way. Anyway, even if they did, there's no reason for them to see you."

Through the shadows came a low wicker from the direction of Aladdin's stable and she felt her confidence flooding back. She was here for Aladdin and being a wimp was not going to help.

Carefully stashing her bike behind the stable block nearest the road, she walked quickly through the velvety darkness across the smooth expanse of tarmac, carrying the sleeping bag in her arms. Her footsteps echoed loudly in her ears, too loudly, and she automatically rose onto her tiptoes, alert for the slightest sound. Something darted across the ground ahead of her and when she heard the squeak of a rat from within the black shadow of the barn wall, a quiver of revulsion made her stomach turn over. She hadn't thought about the rats.

Aladdin was Aladdin. She knew it as soon as she slipped into his stable and the relief was total, for that had been one of her worst fears, arriving only to find that the strange, *other* Aladdin had replaced her precious horse again.

He nuzzled her and she fed him a piece of carrot, reveling in the fact that he was simply himself. She had come here to protect him from the unknown force that somehow threatened them both, believing that just by being here she could keep it at bay. If it had already taken him back into its evil grip she would have been lost before she started.

Once settled down on the straw in the corner of the stable, Laura felt better. What would she do if the

Flynnes found her here? They would think she was completely crazy. She smiled to herself in the darkness. Perhaps she was. But Penny knew. Penny believed in her. The thought was comforting and she found herself wishing once again that she had told her new friend what she intended to do. At least then someone would know she was here if something went wrong. But nothing could go wrong… could it?

Aladdin seemed calm and relaxed, appreciating the company. Every now and then he would move across from his haynet and just nuzzle her gently, as if to reassure himself. Laura flicked on her flashlight, snuggled down into her sleeping bag, and withdrew the magazine from her knapsack. As long as she stayed awake they would be fine, and perhaps tomorrow Penny's book would come up with some clues. She didn't dare allow herself to think beyond that.

At first it was easy. The sounds of the night kept sleep at bay, the hoot of an owl, the ever present squeaking and scuffling of rats. When one came foraging around Aladdin's manger she almost screamed. Stuffing her fist into her mouth she threw her bag in its direction and in a second it was gone, even more afraid than she.

Aladdin snorted in the darkness and as she went across to calm him down.

"It was only me being a wimp," she murmured. "I wasn't throwing it at you."

He tossed his head; blowing softly and as she made

her way back to where her sleeping bag made a dark shape in the straw, a pale beam of light fell across the ground in front of her.

From over the stable door she could see a full moon slipping silently from behind the rapidly disappearing clouds. Suddenly everything was bathed in its magical, silvery light. Way, way above, a million stars sparkled in the navy sky and for a moment Laura stood entranced. The rising wind sang through the treetops, and their swaying branches cast flickering shadows upon the pale gleam of the yard.

She heaved a deep sigh at the beauty of the scene and a kind of calmness settled over her. Everything was going to be all right, she was sure of it. Even Aladdin seemed to be quietly dozing.

Settling comfortably back down into the straw she opened a bag of chips and picked up her magazine again. It would soon be morning.

She didn't see the wild light that gleamed in Aladdin's eye when her eyelids began to droop. Didn't hear the eerie yowl that had even the rats cowering in corners.

The flashlight fell from her limp fingers into the crisp golden straw. Sleep folded over her like a warm irresistible blanket… And the nightmare began again.

Chapter Ten

Fear was a living thing, guiding her every move, totally consuming her senses until all she could do was run from the terror that ripped and tore at her horse's heels.

Storm's muscles bulged as he galloped through the trees and she clung to his mane, her legs clamped around his heaving sides, her skin wet with his sweat.

She knew it was too late, knew that they could not outrun the giant cat that screamed and clawed at their heels. Storm lowered his head, leaping into the air and kicking out at the claws that scoured his sensitive skin. When Laura heard his scream of terror she felt a white-hot anger bubble up inside her, as she clung, helpless, to his heaving body.

Just when she thought that the giant cat would drag them down, something deep inside her fought back and she, too, screamed into the darkness. It was a dream, just a dream.

"Aladdin," she shrieked, but her voice was lost against the fearsome yowling of the great black beast.

"Aladdin!" she screamed again. "Aladdin!"

And suddenly the quivering creature beneath her shuddered to a halt and the screaming stopped.

When she opened her eyes, the blackness was gone and everything was bathed in the silver light of a huge full moon. It was suspended, motionless, in the velvet sky, way beyond a dark network of branches that loomed above her head.

A hysterical gurgle rose in her throat when she felt the cold night air against her face. It really was a dream… just a terribly real dream. But what was she doing here in the woods? How had she come to be here? Was she dreaming still? Would she wake in a moment to find herself back in the stable?

The demon was gone and it was no longer Storm who stood heaving beneath her, but her own dear, familiar Aladdin. So why was she still in the dream?

Tentatively she looked around. The wind whispered through the trees, caressing her face and she could see everything quite plainly in the light of the iridescent moon. What was that just ahead of her? What was that great dark chasm right in front of Aladdin's hooves? She slipped to the ground, realizing vaguely that he wore no tack as she fell to her knees and crept toward its very edge.

She couldn't breathe, couldn't focus, and couldn't grasp the fact that one more step would have sent them both plunging to their doom… for they stood on the very edge of the cliff that loomed above the cave, deep in the center of Faversham Wood.

It wasn't a dream any more, now it was real… a living dream. She had pulled them both out of the nightmare just in time, but what about next time? Next time the demon might win.

Her instinct screamed at her to run to safety. But where was safety? She hesitated. Stark terror and a devastating, empty sense of isolation coursed through her veins, Suddenly it came to her. Faversham Hall, she could go to Faversham Hall.

Beside her Aladdin quivered and her heart contracted when she saw the expression in his eyes. For behind the fear and confusion lurked trust. Aladdin believed in her and she couldn't let him down.

"Come on boy," she said, her voice mind shatteringly loud in the total silence. "I'll look after you."

The journey through the overgrown woodland seemed to last forever. She had taken off her shirt and tied one sleeve around Aladdin's neck as a makeshift lead rope, but every time he jumped or baulked the knot came undone, and she had to re-fasten it. If he panicked and really tried to gallop off she knew she would never be able to hold him so she talked to him all the time, thinking of anything other than nightmares and demons. And in the end it was herself she began to calm down.

As she pushed her way through the dense undergrowth, focusing her whole mind on reaching the pathway, the words just flowed out of her. Silly meaningless sentences, long-forgotten nursery rhymes, and eventually just a melodic, rhythmic chanting – anything to keep her mind away from her nightmare, anything to keep her sane. And when at last she saw it... the gate into the garden of Faversham Hall, her tears began to flow.

Penny Whitmore tossed and turned in her bed. Where was Laura? If only she knew how much danger she might be in. She had phoned Cherry Tree Cottage as soon as she finished reading about the last Lady Faversham but, to her dismay, Laura's father had told her that his daughter was on her way to stay with her. Fortunately Penny covered up immediately for her friend and said nothing to raise alarm or add suspicion. But where was she? What if she had set off to Faversham Hall and never quite got here?

Again and again she decided to call the police, or Laura's parents, anyone who might help. When the clock in the hallway struck three she picked up her cell phone and started to dial. She was on the last digit when she heard a distant, muffled sound and her finger pressed the cancel button as she rushed across to look out of the window.

Below her the garden was swathed in moonlight. It looked far too beautiful to harbor that long-forgotten, lingering evil. A prickle of doubt set in, but before it could take root she saw a movement, a dark shape, something materializing through the trees.

Her heart contracted... froze... and then swelled with relief as the silver moonlight picked out the slight build of Laura. And beside her was Aladdin.

Stifling a whoop of joy she ran silently down the stairs in her bare feet, grabbed her jacket from the peg by the back door, and rushed out into the garden. Her feet hit sharp gravel. She swore under her breath and fumbled for her boots.

She caught up with them just as they reached Cheerful's stable, and without saying a word Penny opened the door. She ushered them in and then flicked on the light. There were two boxes in the old stone building separated by a low partition. She took the end of Aladdin's makeshift lead rope from Laura's stiff fingers and led him into the one she used to store the feed and hay. He followed willingly, seeming to take comfort from the presence of the friendly cob. She left the two horses sniffing noses and turned her attention back to her friend.

Laura stood motionless; her fingers pressed against a jagged scratch on her cheek and when Penny saw the expression in her huge gray eyes, a knot tightened in the bottom off her stomach.

"Here," she urged, pressing her gently down onto a straw bale then she sank down beside her and placed a protective arm around her shoulders.

"You're safe now," she said, her voice firm with a conviction that didn't quite reach her eyes. "Now tell me what happened."

Laura leaned forward, shuddering, her hands clasped across her face.

"The nightmare. It was real. It really happened. We nearly… "

Her voice died out and for several moments she sat in silence, wrestling with the suffocating fear, then she looked up at Penny with a kind of dawning horror.

"I don't know how I got there. I can't remember."

Penny held her gaze, her eyes narrowed now with fierce determination.

"But you beat it, Laura. You were stronger than it. Can't you see?"

For a moment the two friends just stared at each other and then Laura's jaw jutted forward and she clutched Penny's arm.

"Tell me about the book," she insisted. "You've read it, haven't you?"

Penny nodded.

"I'll go and get it, you can see for yourself."

"No."

Laura grabbed Penny's sleeve as she tried to rise, pulling her back down.

"No! Just tell me what you've found out."

Penny hesitated. She had read and re-read the story of the last Lady Faversham a dozen times throughout the endless night until she felt as if the details were embedded in her brain. But now, suddenly, she felt as if she didn't know where to begin. Her forehead puckered into a frown and she passed her tongue nervously across her lips.

Please," urged Laura, and Penny sat heavily back down beside her.

"Look," Penny began. "I've had all night to think about this. A little while ago I'd have laughed if someone tried to tell me about the things that are happening around here, but just listen to the story and then tell me what you think. I know what I believe, and to be honest, it's crazy."

Laura was desperate.

"I just need to get it straight in my head. I need to know what to do."

Penny took a big deep breath and flicked her hair back from her face. Then she began to speak in a low, urgent voice.

"Many years ago Lord and Lady Faversham lived right here in this very house. They had a six-year-old son, Richard, and after her husband was killed in a hunting accident Lady Anne Faversham would hardly let the child out of her sight.

"Witches were commonplace in those days and there was a black witch who lived in and around Faversham Wood; they called her the Black Witch of Faversham. By night she used to take on the guise of a great black cat and prey upon the village children, using their innocent souls for her own evil ends.

"When she took young Richard, his mother was distraught, and she swore that she would never rest until she found him. Hour after hour, night after night, she went out searching mounted upon her favorite horse, a great black stallion named Storm Spirit."

Laura's fingers dug into her arm, but Penny ignored her and carried on with the story.

"The Black Witch chased them to their doom, but

they are said to be searching still. Both she and Storm Spirit have been seen many times, in and around the woods and lanes of Faversham. They will never rest until the child is found."

As her voice died away Laura realized that there were tears on her cheeks and her heart felt as if it was going to burst with the emotions that welled up inside her. But it was the one unanswered question that sent an involuntary shiver through her limbs.

"What happened to the witch?"

Her voice was little more than a whisper.

"What happened to the witch?" she repeated more urgently, and Penny glanced uneasily at the floor before meeting her intense gaze.

"When she took Richard Faversham, the whole village rose up against her and… "

Her voice faltered.

"They sealed her forever in her lair."

Laura felt the evil curl around her as if she was once again outside the cave, and she looked at Penny with a desperate light in her eyes.

"And I released her… It's true isn't it? You believe it too, I can tell by your voice."

"Look," admitted Penny. "I felt just like you do when I first read the story, but I've had all night to get it straight in my head."

She took Laura by the shoulders then and looked straight into her eyes.

"Listen. You fought her off in the woods and you

can fight her off again. She doesn't seem to be able to get to you if you are awake, just remember that, so we have to do something today."

"But what about Aladdin? Why does she want Aladdin?"

Penny dropped her hands to her sides.

"I don't think it is the witch who takes over Aladdin."

"You think its Storm," gasped Laura. "Of course, Storm *Spirit!* Aladdin's registration papers. His sire was called *Spirit* of Fire."

"And they look the same," went on Penny, taken up by her friend's excitement. "That's the link, somewhere, way back, they must be related. Storm is taking over Aladdin to try and get his help."

"Or our help," suggested Laura. "Maybe it was he who made Aladdin bolt that very first day in the forest."

"And made you find the cave," blurted Penny. "He *wanted* you to free the witch so he and Lady Anne could confront her about the child and find out where she put him."

Laura shook her head in disbelief.

"I can't believe we are even saying these things let alone believing them. We'll have to tell someone, get some help."

Penny shrugged hopelessly.

"I've thought that one through, too. Who should we tell? Your parents? My parents? They'd have us both in front of a psychiatrist pretty quick, don't you think?

Or what about Billy Flynne? I can hear him laughing now. No. We are alone in this and there must be a way to stop it."

"We'll just have to get rid of the witch," finished Laura slowly. "But how?"

"First of all, I want you to tell me everything that happened to you tonight," insisted Penny. Then we will find a way. We have to."

Telling Penny every detail of her living nightmare helped Laura. As if by explaining it all to her friend it made the details more clear in her own mind. She *had* fought off the evil, *had* managed to drag herself from the dream just in time and she could do it again if necessary. *But what if you can't,* whispered an inner voice.

When Laura had finished, Penny placed her chin on her palms and shook her head slowly to and fro as if struggling to take it in. Then she dropped her hands onto her knees and looked up at her friend.

"Part of me says that we are both completely nuts and part of me believes that this whole ridiculous thing is true," she said. "And if it is true then it seems to me that the Black Witch of Faversham is getting stronger all the time. We have to find a way to stop her before the night sets in again."

"Well whatever we decide I'll have to go back to Hightor before anyone is up and working," announced Laura. "If they find Aladdin's stable empty and a flashlight and sleeping bag in the straw, they'll probably call both my parents and the police."

"You can't," protested Penny. "You can't ride back through the wood."

A sense of hopelessness flooded Laura and she spread out her hands, palms up.

"What other option do I have?"

"I could go," cried Penny. "I don't think the witch can get to me."

"But you don't know that," said Laura. "No, I have to go, but I'll come back as soon as I can."

"I could come with you," pleaded Penny."

Laura was adamant.

"No. I'll be all right. You stay here and try to think a way to exorcise the witch."

"The library," cried Penny. "There's a library here and some of the books are hundreds of years old. Dad keeps on saying he's going to catalogue them but he never gets around to it. There might be something there that can help us."

Laura's spirits rose.

"Anything," she urged. "Look for anything at all that might be mystical or magical."

"And you'd better gallop as fast as you can through that forest," insisted Penny. "Don't look anywhere but straight ahead."

"Slight problem there," said Laura with the flicker of a smile. "I'm going to need to borrow your tack."

Chapter Eleven

Penny stood motionless in the gateway as the sound of Aladdin's galloping hooves faded into the dark silence of Faversham Wood. Pale moonlight rimmed the trees with silver and moving black shadows in the undergrowth sent a shiver down her spine. But still she waited, trying to gauge the time that Laura would leave the pathway for the lane that led eventually to Hightor and safety – if there was such a thing.

The minutes ticked by and the silence folded around her like a cloak, surely Laura would be there by now. She stepped from the shadowy woodland into the brightness of the garden just as a deep purple cloud floated across the silver moon, plunging everything once again into darkness. She broke into a run, fumbling her way through untended bushes and tripping over tussocks of long grass, until at last she saw the warm yellow beam of light that shone from Cheerful's stable. Her steps slowed, her breath came in great heaving gasps and she leaned forward with her hands on her knees. Laura must be there by now. Just in front of her Cheerful nickered, a soft, gentle, comforting sound, and she looked up with a smile and went across to throw her arms around his neck.

"Every thing is going to be all right," she told him. "I know it."

The library was one of the rooms as yet untouched at Faversham Hall. Sam Whitway insisted that he was leaving it until last. "Just to catalogue the books will be a mammoth task," were his exact words when his wife mentioned it. She had reluctantly agreed, and settled for decorating the dining room instead. When Penny slipped in through the heavy oak door she could almost smell the antiquity of the place. Had Lady Anne Faversham read these books, she wondered. Had she sat in the tall backed chair by the fireplace and read to her doomed son, Richard? The idea made Penny shiver. It wasn't fear that she felt, as much as a deep, overpowering sadness for poor Lady Faversham whose love for her child was so strong that she still searched for him after all these years.

Books lined two walls, stretching from the hardwood floor to the ornate cornice at the high ceiling, and Penny looked up wondering where to start. At the beginning, she decided, moving to the empty wall where a huge window overlooked the countryside.

The dark forest loomed ominously beyond the garden and she caught her breath, turning quickly back toward the books. If she and Laura were to beat this crazy thing, she knew that she had to be strong. The one thing she couldn't allow herself was the luxury of fear, and that fear was rooted in Faversham Wood.

For an hour or more she moved from book to book. There seemed to be everything but what she was looking for: books on art, books on medicine, beautifully bound volumes of poetry, but nothing on the black arts. In a fit of despair at the size of her task she sank down onto the tall backed chair. Whether or not she dozed for a moment she would never know, but when her eyes suddenly snapped open, she thought she heard a swishing sound, like the rustle of silk.

She glanced around the silent room and took a great deep breath as a strange feeling overcame her, a stifling feeling of sadness. It hung in the air, a deep, heavy clinging emotion that made her heart swell inside her chest. She jumped to her feet in confusion.

The early morning sun streamed through the tall window. Beyond the garden the trees of Faversham Wood made a glorious backdrop of vibrant greens and browns; a picture of beauty and serenity. Had she dreamed of black witches and long-dead spirits that could take over the living? If only she had.

When she moved toward the books again, remembering her task, her eyes were irresistibly drawn to the very top row and a strange compulsion made her reach for the steps. She climbed them carefully, stretching upwards for a black bound book that hovered just beyond her reach. As her fingers made contact she heard, once again, the rustle of silk.

Even before she read the title she just knew that she

had the right book. When she looked at the cover her heart began to beat like a drum.

The way of the Witch

And beneath the title, embossed in gold, was a pentacle – the sign of the witch.

Laura had never been so pleased to reach Hightor. To her relief everything was still in darkness. The gate was swinging open, as she must have left it, and when she led Aladdin into his box she saw the flashlight, still shining into the straw. Thank heavens she had gotten here before anyone found Aladdin gone and her belongings abandoned in his box. They would have thought she'd completely lost it, but then again, maybe she had. Perhaps she really had dreamed the whole crazy business.

When she led Aladdin into his stall and began to untack him, the claw marks on his flank came as a rude reminder that it had not been a dream after all. They stood out red and sore, as if freshly done and for the first time it occurred to her that she really did think of them as claw marks now. Inside her head she heard once again the screaming howls of the giant cat that had chased them through the darkness.

"What are we going to do, boy?" she whispered into

the long silky strands of Aladdin's mane. Then she took a big deep breath and tried to be positive. The sooner she could get back to Penny, the sooner they could begin to try and do something. *What?* screamed an inner voice, but she pushed that question firmly into the back of her mind.

When she had bathed Aladdin's cuts and fed him, she rolled up her sleeping bag, put her belongings back into the bag, and left them with her bicycle behind the stable block. By the time old Jim arrived in the yard she was already mucking out as if it were just an ordinary day.

"You're bright and early," he called.

"Early bird catches the worm," she retorted, in such a lighthearted tone that it surprised even her. "I want to get my work done because I'm going to see Penny later."

She went about her tasks on automatic pilot, wondering how she could be doing this after last night. Last night she could have been killed, couldn't she? Forcing the thought away, she worked feverishly until Billy appeared with his usual impish grin, making everything seem just a bit more normal.

"You must have come early," he remarked. "Just as well though, because Dad and I have to go and look at some horses. I'll feed this lot and help with the yards, of course, then we'll have to be off."

As he turned to walk away Laura plunged her fork into the straw again and suddenly his face reappeared around the doorway, making her jump.

"You all right?" he asked with a frown and she forced a wide smile onto her face.

"Of course," she said. "Just a bit tired, that's all."

Two hours later, just before Billy and he left, Mike Flynne arrived carrying a huge plate of bacon buns. He insisted that they all stop for a quick breakfast in the tack room and Laura reluctantly put down her fork. Her stomach turned over at the thought of eating, but she smiled and bit into the soft white bread with feigned delight. It tasted like cotton wool in her mouth as she forced it down. And around her they laughed and joked and made ordinary conversation as if it was just another regular day.

After Billy and his father left with the horsebox she worked in a fury, desperate to get finished. She had to get away, had to find out how Penny was coming along with her quest. Still, she couldn't just leave everything for poor old Jim to do.

Minutes turned to hours, but at last they were done. All the yards were neatly swept, every horse was mucked out and fed, and some of them had been turned out into the meadow behind the stables.

"Better get off, lass," suggested old Jim. "I can see something is eating at you."

His piercing blue eyes shone out at her from within the confines of his weathered face and she hesitated, holding his gaze.

"Do you know anything about the witch that haunts the forest?"

The words, even as she uttered them, took her completely by surprise but the old man just gave her a crooked smile and nodded knowingly.

"Been having dreams?"

Laura froze and he reached out to touch her arm.

"Dreams are all inside your own head you know, lass. They can't hurt you if you just remember that."

"What do you mean?"

She ran behind him as he walked off across the yard shaking his head and muttering to himself.

"Take no notice," he insisted, waving her away with a gnarled hand. "It's just the ramblings of an old man. Now get yourself gone."

They may have been the ramblings of an old man, but they gave Laura confidence as she entered Faversham Wood again. She had intended to go all the way around by the road but that would have taken her hours and it also meant riding along a busy two-way road. Jim's advice and unexpected understanding had given her the strength to face the forest. As she urged Aladdin through the gate she found herself wondering how he knew about the dream. Perhaps he, too, had had dealings with the black witch, but he was still here, wasn't he?

Aladdin seemed calm, the sun was shining, and she felt very positive. Jim was right; dreams really were just inside your own head, she was sure of it. Pushing Aladdin forward into a smart trot she stared straight ahead, refusing to allow herself to look left or right.

"Let's just hope that Penny has found a way," she murmured to Aladdin and he broke into canter, as eager as she to put the eerie atmosphere of Faversham Wood behind them.

Penny sat on a straw bale in the stable block with the book spread out before her. Her eyes devoured page after page and every now and then she stopped to scribble anything that seemed even remotely relevant down onto a pad. The things she learned made her shiver but she kept on reading, searching for clues, anything that might help them in their quest to destroy the Black Witch of Faversham.

When the stable door opened unexpectedly she dropped her pen and looked up with a start.

"Are you back already?" she exclaimed.

"What do you think?" responded Laura with a smile. "It is almost lunchtime I thought you'd have been wondering where I was."

She led Aladdin in through the door and deposited Cheerful's tack on the partition between the two stables.

"What a job I had carrying that," she groaned and Penny threw her a worried glance.

"Are you sure you are all right?"

Laura shrugged. "As all right as anyone could be in my situation. At least Aladdin still seems to be Aladdin and I have ridden through the forest without being chased over the cliff. Have you found anything that might help us?"

Penny's face flushed with excitement and she held out the book.

"Well, I don't know what you'll think, but if you sit down I'll try to show you."

Laura un-tacked Aladdin with slow deliberate movements, suddenly afraid of what she was about to hear.

"Come on," urged Penny, patting the straw bale, and Laura sank reluctantly down beside her, finally allowing her gaze to fall on the leather bound book.

"This," explained Penny, pointing to the motif on the front cover, "is a pentacle, the sign of the witch."

Laura felt a cold finger of fear prickle down her spine as she allowed the reality of what they were doing to sink in.

"The sign of the witch," she repeated in awe, staring at the five pointed star set inside a circle.

"The top one points to the spirits," Penny continued. "And the other four triangular shapes are symbols for the elements: air, earth, water, and fire. Witches often use the elements in their spells because they draw power from them. We are going to use the elements *against* our witch."

"Do you think we really can do it?" whispered Laura. Penny nodded.

"We have to try," she said simply. "I've been looking through this book for hours and I think we can make a spell. The power of good will win over evil, but we have to believe in it. That's the most important thing."

"Old Jim told me that dreams can't hurt you if you remember that they are just inside your own head," said Laura. "I asked him if he knew anything about the witch and he did seem to. Anyway, that's what he told me and it made me feel a lot better."

"Do you want me to show you some of the things I've been reading about?" asked Penny, but Laura shook her head.

"No, I believe you. Just tell me about your plan or spell or whatever it is."

Penny stared thoughtfully at her notepad for a moment, then she looked up with a determined expression on her face.

"The book is full of stories about witches that once lived on the earth. There is one very much like our witch, a black witch who did lots of evil things. One night the whole village rose against her. They went to her lair and made a spell demanding that she show herself. Then they sealed her in and a priest blessed the only entrance so that she could never escape."

"And you think that is what happened to the Black Witch of Faversham," gasped Laura.

Penny nodded slowly.

"Something like that."

"But we don't have a priest."

Penny looked at her friend with a strange light in her green eyes.

"And that is exactly why I have spent hours going through the book," she said. "I have looked at the way witches make spells, I've have read about incidents both successful and unsuccessful, and I think we can make a spell that might work."

Laura tried to speak, but her teeth clamped shut, and Penny reached out and took hold of her arm, understanding her emotion.

"I felt like you at first," she admitted. "But then I got angry. When I thought about all the children, all those innocent souls that the Black Witch stole, I began to feel stronger and stronger. And then I realized that very strength was what would make the spell work."

There was such intensity in Penny's face, that despite her initial reservations, Laura found herself beginning to believe in her friend's plan.

"You'd better tell me about it then," she said.

"We are going to use everything I can think of to make our spell strong," Penny told her. "Love, innocence, emotions like that. It also says that something taken from a victim will add a surge of raw power, because instilled in it will be vengeance. We don't have anything like that, but we do have the power of good on our side. We need to call on all the elements, so we must draw a pentacle on the floor of the cave. At the four points we will place water, earth – although I suppose that will be there already just as air is – and fire. Then we will call on the witch in the name of the elements and demand that she show herself."

Laura felt the breath freeze in her throat.

"And what if she does?" she whispered.

"*When* she does," announced Penny. "We have to call on the element of fire to vanquish her and then we need a word to call on, a strong word that sums up what we are trying to do. We have to write it on a piece of paper, throw it into the flames, and demand by the power of that word that the witch be destroyed."

"Freedom," murmured Laura. "Freedom and love."

"We'll use them both," said Penny.

"And I think I know where we can get something from a victim of the witch," said Laura.

For a moment the two girls just stared at each other in stunned silence. This had gone beyond a game. Now it was real, and they both knew that they had to believe in it totally.

"It is to save you and Aladdin," insisted Penny, and Laura reached out to clasp her hand.

"The bone," she whispered. "The horse's bone that Toby found beside the cave. I think it might have belonged to Storm."

Penny nodded.

"Then we'll find it and use it. Oh, and there is just one more thing… It is said that a witch's spirit can never die. If you chase it out of one domain (that's what they call the creature or person it lives in), it will find another. It may be a person or it may be a beast, but it will find something or someone."

Laura forced a smile onto her face.

"Well as long as it's far away from here and no longer has power, I suppose that's the best we can hope for."

A heavy silence fell as the two girls contemplated their plan. Laura was the first to break it.

"You know," she admitted. "I can't really believe that we are actually going to do this."

"It is you who will have to do it," Penny told her. "You are the one she is targeting. You are the one she tried to chase over the cliff."

Laura shuddered.

"When will I have to do it?"

"At the witching hour," whispered Penny. "On the stroke of midnight."

Chapter Twelve

Laura's heart turned over the moment she walked into Aladdin's stable and saw the all too familiar, wild light in his great dark eyes. Her steps faltered and the color drained from her face.

"He's here," she whispered. "Storm… he's here."

"Penny stepped up beside her.

"Maybe that's good," she said, her voice tight with forced determination. "Whatever happens we have to take Aladdin with us; he is as much a part of this as you are, and if Storm's spirit is with him, then it must make us stronger."

Laura's fingers clenched and unclenched.

"But I have to ride him."

"Look," Penny walked over to where Aladdin – or Storm – was tossing his head and gazing wildly beyond them toward Faversham Wood. She ran her hand down his gleaming neck. "He's on our side remember, and Aladdin is still here somewhere, you'll see."

Laura felt the pressure of tears behind her eyelids.

"But where is he?" she cried.

"He is still Aladdin, really," insisted Penny. "Here, look, touch him. It's just that Storm's spirit is so strong it can take him over. Come on, it's almost 11 o'clock. We have to go."

Laura placed her hand on the tense muscles of Aladdin's crest and reached up to touch his face. He ignored her, staring out of the door with the wild, distant light in his eyes.

"I'm ready," she said with resignation. "I'll get him tacked up."

Both girls had agreed as nighttime began to fall, that it had been the longest afternoon of their lives. They had gone through their plan again and again, perfecting every detail. But when Laura rang home to say that she was staying at Penny's house again it had almost fallen apart. Her mother, at first, said no. It had taken more than a bit of pleading and promising to persuade her, and when she did finally succumb to her daughter's pleas, Laura felt momentarily disappointment.

"You must try to get stronger," Penny had insisted, recognizing her reluctance. "You have to believe in what we are going to do or it will never work. Just think of Aladdin, think of the dreams, think of that cliff… think of all those poor children and Richard Faversham."

"I know," insisted Laura.

And she had tried. All the time they were gathering up the things they were going to need, she had tried, but up until now it hadn't really worked. Not until this moment.

The moon cast a silver light across the world, a silver light that shone in her horse's eyes. Suddenly she was filled with a terrible anger.

"We have to do this," she murmured. "We have to stop her."

They set off through the trees in silence, both aware of the enormity of the task ahead of them. Penny had all the things they needed in a backpack and her lips were set in a grim line as she followed Aladdin along the pathway. Only Cheerful seemed unaffected by the atmosphere. He was, as always, just Cheerful. He grabbed at the undergrowth as they pushed their way into the dense woodland and Penny kicked him forward as Aladdin increased his pace.

Laura's worst fear was that she wouldn't be able to find the cave in the darkness, but she needn't have worried. As soon as they entered the woodland Aladdin – or Storm, as he seemed to be now – took charge, setting his jaw against the bit and fighting his rider's commands. In the end Laura gave him full control. His ears were sharply pricked as he pushed his way through the undergrowth, and she wrapped her fingers into his long mane as the darkness consumed them. She tried to keep her anger going, keeping an attempt to sustain her strength. And then at last she could see the moon again, floating above them in the clear, dark purple sky. When the horse beneath her stopped and raised his head, snorting his defiance into the looming shadows, there was no question in Laura's mind that he truly was Storm Spirit. Her heart ached for Aladdin, swelling the festering anger, and she looked with new eagerness toward the cave.

"There it is," she whispered, slipping to the ground.

"Come on then," urged Penny, already securing Cheerful's lead rope to a tree. But when Laura tried to follow suit Aladdin reared, rebelling against the constriction.

"Leave him," insisted Penny. "He knows what he's doing."

Letting her precious horse stand alone and free in the center of the clearing was, for Laura, an act of total faith, a true sign that she really did believe in all this.

"Hurry," Penny urged. "Where can we find that bone of yours?"

They worked fiercely on the mound of stones. Laura had brought a small flashlight and it flickered across the pile of rubble – rubble that had lain undisturbed for hundreds of years – until Toby decided to dig underneath it.

"It must have been a landslide from the top of the cliff," whispered Penny and beside her Laura nodded in the darkness.

"Maybe it happened when Storm fell," she suggested, and for a moment Penny froze.

"Do you think he is still lying under here… all of him? I thought we were just looking for one little bone."

"Wouldn't his bones have disintegrated by now?"

Laura shrugged, taking a firm grip of her friend's arm.

"You hear of people finding skeletons from thousands of years ago if the conditions are right. Billy was convinced it was a horse's bone that Toby found. If you think about it, after the cave was sealed no one would have come here for years. I suppose this place was just overgrown and forgotten."

Behind them Storm snorted, tossing his head as if in approval, and they redoubled their efforts.

When they found the long heavy object Laura felt suddenly weak, knowing immediately what it was.

"This will do," she cried, hauling it from its resting place.

When the skull lay on the ground in front of them Laura ran the beam of her flashlight across it. She heard Penny gasp, reflecting her own sense of awe that the remains of Storm Spirit really did lie here. That beautiful black horse had plunged to his death at this very place all those years ago. And his rider…

Laura grasped hold of the object, feverishly scraping the dirt from it.

"Come on," she urged. "We haven't much time."

There was a strange smell in the cave – an evil, stagnant smell, like something long dead. An icy cold made Laura pull her jacket more closely around herself. As she ran her flashlight over the damp walls, the breath caught in her throat. She pointed the beam of light at Penny's face revealing ashen cheeks and huge round eyes that seemed to envelop her whole face.

"You look as scared as I feel."

The words came out in a strangled squeak, and Penny responded with a forced grin.

"That's because I am," she admitted. "Let's just get it over with."

With great reverence they placed the horse's skull in the very center of the cave. Penny tipped out the contents of her bag and picked up a short pointed stick.

"Here," she said, passing it to Laura. "You'll have to do it."

Laura had practiced drawing a pentacle time and again that afternoon, and now she drew the shape with sure strokes. First the circle, and then within it, the triangular shapes that made up the five-pointed star. For the elements they had brought water, which they poured into a small wooden bowl. Earth, hastily gathered by Laura from where they found the skull, and for the fire they were going to use dried holly because it was supposed to have special powers. To make sure that it burned, Penny had soaked it in oil. As Laura stacked it into a neat pile on the third point of the star, she fumbled in her pocket, heaving a sigh of relief as her fingers closed around the matchbox. The fourth point they left empty because air was already present, and the fifth pointed to the entrance, to call on the spirits.

"There."

Laura sat back on her haunches, surveying her handiwork then she looked up at Penny.

"What time is it?"

"Almost midnight."

They stood then, in the very center of their pentacle, taking strength from each other's closeness. Laura closed her eyes to suppress the raw panic that swept through her body.

Penny grasped her hand tightly.

"Think about the children," she whispered. "And Aladdin."

Laura remembered the sections that Penny had read aloud from the book that afternoon, the sections she had repeated to herself over and over until they were imprinted on her brain. She raised her arms, focusing her mind on the task ahead, waiting for the power to come, willing it to control her.

She knew that she had to take strength from the elements, so she imagined a storm-driven wind howling through the trees, the warm earth beneath her feet, and crystal clear water crashing down onto the rocks. And at last she felt it, creeping throughout her whole body in a glorious surge, bringing with it such a sense of purpose that she began to chant the words they had chosen. She reached out to Penny for the lighted taper with total confidence.

Once it was in her grasp, she touched it to the holly branches.

Like a living thing the fire crackled into life and as the flames spiraled up into the air she raised her hands once more. Her voice took on an unworldly, chanting ring.

"By the power of the elements I call on you, Black Witch of Faversham."

She held her hands toward the curling flames, her eyes glowing amber in the firelight. Then she stooped to take a handful of earth, sprinkling it through her fingers.

"By the power of the earth I call on you."

In her hand she cupped some water from the wooden bowl and trickled it over the skull. *"By the power of water I call on you."*

Then she made a circle in the air and closed her eyes, breathing deeply.

"By the power of the air I call on you."

For a moment there was total silence before she turned again toward the fire.

"By the power of fire, Black Witch of Faversham, I demand that you show yourself."

Penny sank back against the hard rock face as a roaring sound rent the air, but Laura stood fast, staring at the spiral of smoke that rose above the flames.

"By the power of fire, Black Witch of Faversham, I demand that you show yourself," she repeated.

The smoke began to form itself into a shape, a shape that writhed and screamed above the flames. First the form was that of a person. Then it began to change, and as it did, the screaming turned to a snarling, hissing yowl. The sounds of the giant cat from the nightmare… the cat from hell.

Amber eyes glowed in its broad black head like living coals. Its huge jaws opened wide, revealing vicious, pointed fangs that flashed white in the firelight. It sank down onto its haunches, poised to pounce, poised to tear Laura limb from limb, but she stood her ground. Hands raised high above her head she stared unflinchingly at the evil demon.

"In the name of all that is good and holy, Black Witch of Faversham, I vanquish thee."

The great black beast yowled once more, but this time there was just the slightest recoil as Laura stepped confidently toward it, arms outspread. Keeping her eyes firmly locked with those of the cat, she dropped the first slip of paper into the flames. As the word written upon it burned she raised her voice until it echoed around the cave.

"By the power of love, Black Witch of Faversham, I demand you be gone from this place."

When she held the second slip of paper near the fire, the great black demon sank down onto its haunches. The flames curled around the word she had so carefully written, and the beast let out a piercing scream.

"By the power of freedom, Black Witch of Faversham, I destroy thee," she cried.

The word echoed around the cave. *Freedom... freedom... freedom.* For one long, frozen moment, Penny was sure that the cat was going to strike. It squirmed and twisted, screeching in pain and anger. And then it was gone. In the flash of a million lights it vanished, fading from sight as the last flame flickered and died. In the blackness that descended there was total silence. Time stood still, and without conscious thought both girls stood completely motionless, waiting for they knew not what.

Laura wilted as the power drained from her body. Her shoulders slumped but still she waited and into her head, unbidden, came the warning from the book.

A witch's spirit can never die, but only moves from one domain to another, be it man or beast.

For one fleeting moment an awful premonition flooded over her and then she heard the sound that dispelled all fear… the joyous, tinkling laughter of a hundred happy children.

As the sound rippled through the cave, Penny stepped up close to Laura and the two girls clung together in awe. Shimmering images of little children appeared. They were running toward the moonlit night, reaching out with chubby fingers to grasp their freedom.

And when they were gone a small light still shone from the darkness, a light that picked out one last child. He was standing motionless, staring toward the entrance, his angelic features alight with such happiness that both girls felt the tears roll silently down their cheeks. And then he, too, ran toward the freedom of the night, passing through them as if they weren't there. Penny and Laura followed in his footsteps, knowing where they led.

Across the clearing, rimmed with moonlight, stood a great black horse and on its back, her face aglow with an ethereal light, sat the lady from the painting. The child ran to her, his hair a shimmering halo in the

light of the moon. In one smooth movement she reached out her arms and scooped him up.

The great black horse spun around but she reined him in, looking across the clearing toward the cave and for one long moment she held Laura's gaze, her lips curved into a gentle smile of gratitude.

As they watched in wonder, the image of horse and rider began to fade, until at last there was just an empty space beneath the tree where the last Lady Faversham had been. The two girls stood speechless, their arms about each other.

"Come on," whispered Penny at last. "Let's go home."

They rode home in silence through the peaceful woodland, without any trace of fear to mar their journey. Later they would talk, but for now they were both content with their thoughts, unable yet to find the words to describe their experience. Aladdin was Aladdin again, forever, and the children were free. That was enough for now.

Conclusion

As Laura rode slowly along the pathway on her way to Hightor, she heard the sweet trill of birdsong and looked up with delight to see that life had returned to the once silent woodland. There was a new atmosphere about the whole place, a peacefulness, and she found herself humming in time with the wind that sang in the trees above her head.

It seemed strange to be doing such a normal thing as riding to Hightor after last night. To be going about her usual routine, as if it was just another ordinary day.

"I suppose life goes on," she had said to Penny as she left Faversham Hall that morning. And Penny had simply smiled and handed her Aladdin's reins.

"Just be glad that it can," she advised.

Aladdin stepped out from the wood into the bright autumn sunshine and headed along the lane toward Hightor. Laura allowed him to wander on a loose rein. She felt totally drained of energy, her face was pale and drawn, but a glow of inner happiness shone from her eyes. Last night she and Penny had talked until dawn, trying to come to terms with their experience. The truth of it was that there was no way they would ever be able to come to terms with it. But the witch was gone and the children were free. Now they could get on with their lives.

Beyond the hedge she could see the roof of Cherry Tree Cottage. Her mother would be making breakfast before her father went off to work. Or, she might be standing at the sink in the kitchen window, up to her elbows in soapsuds.

Life goes on, Laura thought again, and she suddenly found herself longing for the comfortable normalcy of home. She wanted to see her mother and look around at the things she knew; just to be sure that nothing had changed.

She glanced at her watch. There was time to stop by. She would just pop in and say hello.

Aladdin faltered as she rode along the narrow drive to the front door, but she urged him on, turning down the side of the house to the back door where her father had fitted a ring in the wall.

"Won't be long," she promised, leaving him firmly tied by his lead rope. He tossed his head and snorted nervously as she pushed the back door open.

Her mother was, as expected, by the sink.

"Hello sweetheart," she called. "Oh! Go and have a look in the sitting room. I have a surprise for you."

Laura smiled.

"What is it?"

"See for yourself," insisted her mother.

She stepped into the warmth of the comfortable, familiar room. A fire burned in the grate, its newly-lit flames crackling up the chimney. Laura's gaze focused on the dark shape that preened itself before the hearth.

With leisurely arrogance it turned to look at her, its glowing amber eyes burning into her very soul. She felt the breath being sucked from her body.

"Isn't it a gorgeous cat?" came her mother's voice from behind her. "It woke me up soon after midnight, scratching on the door. I do hope it will stay."